About the Book

Paris in the spring was about the last place in the world that thirteen-year-old Michael Horner wanted to be. Miserable attending *l'École des Petits Étrangers* (or, as Michael put it, The School of the Little Strangers), he would have done just about anything to be back home in Bend, Oregon. But his father was doing research and his mother and sister were delighted with the French shops and museums, so Michael didn't seem to have much choice.

Until one day he took matters into his own hands and quit school to become an authority on gargoyles! Through a telescope his father has given him Michael observes the gargoyles ornamenting the top of the Cathedral of Notre Dame and even makes friends with the most amiable. But it isn't until late one night that Michael notices the most special gargoyle of them all—the gargoyle that could only be described as pretty!

Everyone knows that there is no such thing as a pretty gargoyle. So Michael sets out to discover who or what this creature could possibly be. Before he is through, he has been chased through Paris by *les flics* (the cops), discovered an unsuspected talent, and had a surprising change of heart about several things. William Corbin's fans have a lighthearted, fast-paced treat in store with his newest book.

THE PRETTIEST GARGOYLE

THE PRETTIEST GARGOYLE

by

WILLIAM CORBIN

Pseud. William C. McGraw

Coward, McCann & Geoghegan, Inc.
New York

Contents

THE PRETTIEST GARGOYLE

1

An Unwanted
Gift

"Why have I got to get *culture?*" Michael demanded of
his sister, Lucinda, who hadn't said anything at all.

He gave her plenty of time to reply, and when she
didn't, he added in a tone of crushing scorn, "Culture-
shmulture!"—an exclamation so unfunny it would have
informed anyone who knew him how really desperate
Michael was to stir things up.

Lucinda, seated at the wobbly little desk she insisted on
calling an escritoire, kept right on scribbling in her diary.

Michael tried again. "Know what you are? You're a
culture vulture!"

Her silence continued. Somtimes she could make things
awfully difficult for him. While she visibly refrained from

watching, he tore a page from *Paris-Presse* and folded it into a paper airplane. (Paper airplanes at *his* age? Pure desperation!) Then he flung open the tall glass doors to the tiny balcony and sent the little plane swooping out toward the Quai de Montebello. For a moment it looked as if it would swoop clear out over the river Seine, but just then a wind swirled up from no-telling-where and sent it gliding and dipping around the corner, where it disappeared into the Rue de la Bucherie.

"Mike-*ulll!* Will you for heaven's sake *shut the door!*"

He allowed himself the luxury of ignoring *her* for a time, but there was little satisfaction in it, knowing that he really shouldn't leave the door open, chilly as it was and the apartment so costly to heat. Nor did the pleasure of having stirred Lucinda up last long.

The slam of a door told him she had gone to her room to spare herself further sight of him. But just to prove to himself (who else?) that he wouldn't be dictated to by her, he stayed where he was, with the window doors wide open and the chill air swooping around him. Propping his elbows on the balcony's wrought-iron railing, he stared with mounting dejection across the quay and the Seine to the Île de la Cité where the great south tower of the Cathedral of Notre Dame loomed square and solid and everlasting, dominating everything.

He went on staring at the cathedral for a long time while the afternoon grew grayer, wondering over and over if anyone had ever died of being homesick.

Michael Horner was a more or less regulation American boy, age thirteen, with a more or less regulation set of parents, an altogether regulation (meaning unbearable) older sister, age fifteen, and more than regulation collection of problems. The largest of these by a country mile was the fact that he was in Paris, France, where he didn't want to be, instead of in Bend, Oregon, where he did.

Here he was, looking across the Seine to the Cathedral of Notre Dame, when he wanted like fiery hunger to be looking across the Deschutes River to where the humpy backbone of the Cascade Mountains rose high to the west above the pine-forested plateau of central Oregon.

Up there in those mountains where the pines gave way to the firs, the ski slopes would be a dazzling white beneath the May sun. Maybe right now—this very minute—the troop would be up on the practice run at Hoodoo, and Big Sam Lofgren, who was Scoutmaster, would be putting the guys through their paces.

Or maybe it wouldn't be ski practice day, in which case at about this time of evening he'd be unsaddling Canuck out in the stable, giving him a good rubdown, and the steam would be rising from the dark patch of sweaty hide where the saddle blanket had been, and the good horse smell rising with it. . . .

"Well, Mike—*centime* for your thoughts."

Michael jumped as Dad's voice yanked him clear across a continent and an ocean in a split second. The shock was so disconcerting that he let an impoliteness get away from him, bursting out, "Oh, no! You *too!*"

Professor Horner blinked the long slow blink that proved he was really paying attention. "Me too what?" he mildly inquired.

"Oh, *you* know," Michael said, feeling like a sulky six-year-old, but not knowing how to stop. "*Centime* instead of penny. Like Cindy—she can't just go to the *library*, for gosh sakes, she goes to the *bibliothèque*. Or Mom—she's *got* to say *école de cuisine* instead of *cooking school*. It's—well, it's—"

Professor Horner was already nodding. "An affectation. You're right, of course, but try not to be too harsh with us—it's a pretty harmless affectation." He looked inquiringly around, as if just noticing where he was, and took a backward step. "Stuffy of me—but would you mind coming in and shutting the doors!"

With a guilty start Michael obeyed, and his father folded his angular length into an altogether inadequate chair, setting down beside him the big green felt bag in which he carried books and papers to and from the library at the Sorbonne, where he was doing research for his book. Slapping the pockets which used to contain his pipe and tobacco pouch, he made a rueful face and got out instead the roll of Lifesavers that had been with him ever since he stopped smoking. "No more peace pipe," he said, holding the roll out, and while Michael accepted one, he added hopefully, "We could powwow a little anyway."

Michael shrugged. "What's the use! Nothing's any different from last time. I still don't like it here. I never will."

The professor slid the Lifesavers back into the pocket of his tweed jacket. "Never is a long time," he said. "And things change. *We* change."

Michael jammed his hands deep into his pockets, feeling his back stiffening. It wasn't fair he should always have to defend himself. Why shouldn't other people defend *them-*selves now and then! "Well, gosh, if I was going to change, I'd have done it by now, wouldn't I? We've been here four whole months!"

Dad sighed. "If you'd only let your guard down a little, Mike! Give Paris half a chance and she'll get to you."

Michael didn't answer. What was the use? They'd been all through this about a thousand times. Paris was great for Dad. He'd lived here before, in his student days, and spoke the language easily. And it was important that he live here now, to do his research and write his book about thirteenth-century French something or other. It was great for Mom, too, because she'd been born in Singapore and had been traveling off and on ever since, besides being a kind of nut on French cooking and studying about it at the school here. And Cindy, of course. She was clear overboard about art and was going to be the next Grandma Moses or something. Between the two of them they had dragged him through about nine thousand miles of museum and art gallery corridors and so many dismal old churches and palaces that he had moss growing all over him. They'd made him sit through every kind of concert there was—from the opera and huge symphony orchestras to a bunch of funny-looking guys with castanets on their toes playing tunes on what must have been old cigar boxes. If there was anything cultural in the whole city of Paris they hadn't done, it must have been something that was held at the bottom of the Seine. At 4 A.M.

Even worse than all that, though, was the school to which, in a figurative sense, he had to be driven kicking and screaming every weekday. Not a regular school at all. It was a private monstrosity run by a middle-aged English couple named Major and Mrs. Beddoes. Since it was run for the unfortunate offspring of English, American, and Canadian parents living temporarily in Paris, the Beddoeses had named it *l'École des Petits Étrangers*, and since Michael found it easier to translate the last word as "strangers" instead of "foreigners," he always thought of it as the school of the Little Strangers, which sounded particularly icky.

One of the principal functions of the school, according to the brochure which had sold Mom on it in the first place, was to teach all the Little Strangers to speak French fluently. There was no question that the major (known behind his back as the Minor League Major) knew almost everything there was to know about the French language. The problem was that when he spoke it, it was incomprehensible. He sounded the same as he did when he spoke English, and when he spoke English, he sounded like an overloaded garbage disposer which forcibly ejected all in one piece about every seventh word while gargling with the rest of them. The effect, while interesting, didn't communicate very much. Fortunately Mrs. Beddoes, who at least could make herself understood, took over the classes whenever the major was deranged—which he ususally was on Mondays.

The derangement of the major was the result of a deliberate mistranslation by the Little Strangers. What Mrs. Beddoes said was "The major is indisposed this morning," translating it immediately into French: *"Il est dérangé."* And since even the youngest of the pupils learned eventually to associate the major's absences with the splendid plum color of his nose, it was no surprise that whole generations of Little Strangers grew up using the English word "deranged" as a synonym for "hung-over."

The major's nose, unfortunately, was the only bright spot in the whole school, which seemed otherwise uniformly dismal and gray, like the skies over Paris that spring.

That was another source of Michael's general dissatisfaction—the weather. What did it matter if everyone said this had been a very unusual winter and spring? Here it was May, and still the cloud mass hung low aloft, refusing sullenly to move along, while below, the great stone city hunkered down on the banks of its lead-colored river, spiritless and sad.

Michael had turned a little now and was staring dully out the window, forgetting there had been a sort of conversation going, when he heard the very small sound that meant Dad was tactfully trying to turn a deep sigh into something like a normal breath. This was followed in mildly humorous tone with: "Well, powwow adjourned, I guess—for lack of subject matter." His chair made a scraping noise. Then, "Hey—I forgot! Brought you something."

Michael turned to see his father bending over the book bag, his lanky frame looking like an *L* turned upside down. As he untied the bag's drawstring, Michael watched with a kind of wary anticipation. Dad's ideas about gifts could be pretty weird sometimes.

After a moment the professor straightened with a grunt of satisfaction and held up a small brass telescope of the kind that Captain Horatio Hornblower used when he sailed into battle against one of Bonaparte's two-deckers. "Spyglass!" he announced, rather unnecessarily. "Antique, but in excellent condition. Very powerful. *'Une longue-vue très puissante,'* the shopkeeper told me."

"Gee," said Michael. "Well—gee!" What *was* a person supposed to say when his father presented him with an antique spyglass that he needed about as much as he needed a case of the measles.

"I remembered how keen you used to be on bird watching," Professor Horner went on. "You and—uh—Victor Nugent."

Michael sighed, feeling as he frequently did that *he* was the father around here. It was typical of the professor, who seldom could remember what he'd had for lunch, to remember about Victor Nugent and bird watching. It had happened two whole summers ago and had lasted about a month. But now that he'd thought of it, the professor was convinced Michael was a lifelong bird watcher.

He went on about it enthusiastically. "When the good weather comes—and it will, it will—you can jump on the metro and go over to the Bois de Vincennes. Plenty of good bird watching over there, I'd imagine. Besides, there's a fine zoo, and four lakes, and the chateau, of course. Now *there's* a place that's loaded with history—absolutely loaded! Nearly all the French kings lived there while they hunted in the forest. And Henry the Fifth of England died there. And you know what? They *boiled* his body in the chateau kitchen before they sent it back to London to be.

Like everybody in Professor Horner's family, Michael was expert at nipping lectures in the bud. Plucking the old telescope gently from his father's still-outstretched hand, he peered at it for a moment, not altogether without interest. For some reason the weight of it surprised him, and it did look rather *puissant*, though, of course, there was no way of knowing that soon it would turn his whole life around and point it in a new direction. Hurriedly he clapped it to his right eye and through the window swept an arc of imaginary horizon. It was imaginary because the instrument hadn't been focused, and all he could see was a gray blur. That didn't matter; the object was to get Dad out of the Chateau of Vincennes and whatever century he was about to get himself lost in.

"Wow!" Michael exclaimed, nobly tampering with the truth. "It really brings things up close! I sure do thank you. I'll be able to see all kinds of birds with this."

"I thought you'd be pleased," the professor said, sounding pleased himself. "One thing you'll have to get used to, though."

Michael could tell without looking at his father's face that a joke was on its way. "What's that?" he asked cooperatively.

"The birds will sing all their songs in French."

Michael managed a small chuckle. It was right, the way Mom put it: "Your father's jokes all wear little caps and gowns. They're *professorial*."

They could hardly be anything else, Michael thought. Dad *was* a professor, after all—the youngest full professor at Central Oregon College, and head of the History Department besides. Of course, it was a fairly new college and not a very big one, but it was growing, everybody said. For one thing, it was growing straight up the side of its own little mountain just west of Bend, where the Deschutes River foamed its way through the center of town, salmon leaping between the rocks. And from the window of Dad's office you could look westward to the snow caps of the Three Sisters, and north of them to where Three-Fingered Jack thrust its jagged fist into the sky. . . .

Once more the city of Paris faded away, and Michael, without even his own permission, was yearning again for home. To avoid having to talk anymore, he went on pretending to look through the blurry spyglass, and after a little while his father went quietly away. As his step receded, the first deep velvety-thundering bell note of the Angelus came rolling across the river, followed quickly by other notes. The bells of Notre Dame de Paris were calling the devout to prayer as they had been doing for eight hundred years and more.

2

Michael in Revolt

It was the evening of the second day of May when Michael Horner became the owner of the spyglass Longue-Vue Très Puissante. That night while he slept, spring came at last to Paris.

Even before he opened his eyes with the light of the new day's dawn, he knew some kind of miracle had taken place. He could feel it in the air, smell it, taste it almost, and even through closed eyelids he could see it. It was sunlight! His eyes snapped open, and he looked around a room that was only superficially the same as the one he'd gone to sleep in. It was the living room of the apartment they were renting from a Sorbonne professor of archaeology who had gone off to dig things up on some island in the

Mediterranean. Since there were only two bedrooms, Michael had to sleep on the ornate but lumpy sofa that stood at right angles to the tiny fireplace above which a pair of once-gilded swans supported a marble mantel with their bowed necks. Always before, the swans had looked faded and slightly ill against the background of weary-beige wallpaper that framed the fireplace, but now with the light of a brand-new sun slanting through the glass doors from the balcony they seemed fresher and more vigorously swan-like. Even the bearded old gentleman whose ornately framed portrait hung above the mantel had stopped glaring haughtily down and had a glint in his eye that was downright friendly.

All over Michael's body muscles tensed, a million tiny nerves giving them commands while his brain pretended it didn't know what was about to happen. Then it did happen. In a single movement he flung the covers aside and exploded to his feet in the middle of the room, a stringy, reaching figure of a boy with a wild mass of hair the hue of pencil shavings and striped pajamas whose cuffs had long since lost communication with his wrists and ankles.

His bare feet made no sound on the archaeology professor's Oriental rugs, but he tiptoed anyway and opened the balcony doors in careful silence. Ordinarily he had no particular scruples against waking his family up, but the moment now at hand was not one to be shared with anyone; it was for him alone.

Out on the balcony he took a deep breath—part air, part sunshine—and let it out fast so that he could have another. Then he looked up, and there was the sky. Its emptiness, more silver than blue, made him feel that a vast, oppressive weight had been lifted, as if he had been carrying something heavy around on his head—like a birdbath upside down. Or like those swans in there with their marble mantelpiece. Poor swans. Next he looked toward the source of all this resplendence, squinting against the glare. Passing low over the Île St. Louis, the rays of the rising sun glanced off the massive south façade of Notre Dame, turning its heretofore-dead gray stone into a substance shimmering and alive, then brushed through the tops of the trees that lined the Seine embankment, skipped diagonally across the river and the Pont de l'Archevêché (Bridge of the Archbishopric) to arrive triumphantly at Michael's balcony, where they received the kind of welcome that must have made the trip worthwhile.

The air was chilly, but still the sun touched Michael's face with a warmth that was only half imaginary, and when the sudden whir of bicycle tires below brought his gaze down to the level of the street, he couldn't resist calling out to the black-bereted cyclist in his Paris-blue coveralls and wishing him a good morning—along, of course, with a comment on the weather. *"Bon jour, m'sieu! Il fait beau ce matin—oui?"*

The man, now passing directly below the balcony, looked up, startled at being addressed so unexpectedly and so early by a young voice with a foreign accent. For a moment Michael thought he was going to be snubbed for his presumption; then the dark upturned face broke itself in two with a grin as brilliant in its way as the rebirth of the sun, and the man flipped Michael a friendly salute, calling out, *"Tu parles vraiement, mon vieux!"*

In a moment he disappeared, whirring off up the street with a bit of Michael tagging happily along, like a friendly pup. Because the man had addressed him as "old man," which was very friendly indeed, he didn't mind at all the *tu*, which was supposed to be reserved for children. Michael considered himself old enough to be called *vous*, but then how could the man tell the age of a boy on a balcony five stories above his head?

This encounter, trivial though it was, seemed a promising beginning to what couldn't be anything but a marvelous day, and a second later he was struck by a sudden idea which he lost no time putting into effect. Again opening the doors with caution, he went in and reappeared quickly with Old Longview. This name for the spyglass resulted from his practice of translating French words literally into English. Longue-Vue; Longview. Or the Little Strangers and the deranged major. Mainly it was a sort of game designed for the ignoble purpose of annoying Lucinda, who considered it an extremely uncultured thing to do. She was most satisfyingly infuriated, for example, when he referred to the Rue de la Bucherie, the tiny street on which the apartment fronted, as Butchery Street.

At any rate, the spyglass was now Old Longview, and at the moment Michael had a use for it. His eye had caught, far off to the north above the still-shadowy city, the brilliant white domes of the Basilica of Sacré Coeur. He recognized it because there was nothing like it in all Paris—or probably anywhere else. And anyway it was the highest object anywhere to be seen, crowning as it did the hill of Montmartre. (Martyr Mountain, when it came time to annoy Lucinda.) He had been there with her and Mom—in the rain, of course—and it had been a complete bore. But this was different. This was his idea—and his morning—and his telescope. He put the instrument to his right eye, aimed it at Sacré Coeur, and turned the focusing ring.

For a while everything zigged and zagged around in a sort of underwater blur, and then, with the dramatic abruptness of the first picture to appear on a blank television screen, the church leaped into view right in front of his balcony. He drew a quick, startled breath. Old Long-view deserved its name; it was far more powerful than he had guessed. There in front of him was the big dome and the two smaller ones flanking it, all a dazzling white, all looking like egg cups turned upside down, and each sur-mounted by its columned cupola crowned by a golden cross. It seemed almost as if he could throw a rock and bounce it off the big dome's steep sides, or yell and be heard by anyone who might be standing between the cupola's columns.

This flight of fancy gave him a new idea, and he put aside the telescope to look for signs of life near at hand. He was rewarded shortly by the sight of a black-clad figure slowly descending the stairs that led from the island end of the Petit Pont down to the river's edge just below the statue of Charlemagne in front of Notre Dame. Quickly Michael put Old Longview to his eye, aimed, focused, and—presto!— there he was, face to face with a bent but sturdy old man who carried in one hand a fishing pole, and in the other a red string bag from which protruded a wine bottle and a loaf of bread of the long, thin kind known as a *baguette*. Around a fiercely bristling mustache the old man's face was a leathery network of seams that spoke of a lifetime's exposure to wind and weather. He wore his beret tilted to one side, and a mass of white curls bristled from the other. He wore one of those shapeless blue-black suits that seemed to be the unofficial uniform of old men in Paris.

Turning the focusing ring a fraction, Michael brought the face into still-clearer view. Beneath the overhanging mustache the old man's lips were moving as he talked to himself, and the unmistakable eagerness in his eyes as he peered toward his goal, the raised ledge along the stone embankment, was rather sad. Michael felt a touch of shame, as if he were intruding into a stranger's private thoughts. But he went on watching while the old man reached his destination, set the string bag down on a paving stone, and lowered himself laboriously to the ledge above the water, his legs hanging over the edge. With infinite care he unwound the line from the pole, baited the hook with something he took from a little tin box, and lowered it into the water. Then he spoke to the line—or maybe it was to the god of the Seine, if there was one, or to the fish that might come to his hook.

Michael found himself wishing he could read lips in French, but of course he couldn't read them even in English. His imagination presented him with a picture of the old man watching the skies day after day, week after gloomy week, maybe getting up nights in some little room and padding to the window to look for stars. His fishing pole would be standing in the corner, ready for the big moment when it came. And now—some time during the night just past—it *had* come. Michael recalled Dad's laughing about the Seine fishermen. "If anyone ever catches a fish over five inches long," he had said, "the government will probably declare a national holiday." But all the same the old man was here, ever hopeful. And who could tell? On a morning such as this a fish almost as big as a Chinook salmon might come along any moment. The old man's line would tighten as the hook was grabbed, and—

"Michael, what *are* you doing?"

Michael snatched the spyglass from his eye, and the dawn's glory faded as he whirled angrily to face his sister. "Nothing! And why've you got to come sneaking up on me?" His anger was partly the natural reaction of anyone violently startled, the rest because he felt Lucinda was

intruding on something private. Besides, she was laughing
at him. Well, not exactly laughing, but smiling in that
superior way of hers that implied nothing he ever did
could be really important.

She looked a little startled herself, partly because her
long dark hair, still uncombed, was bunchy and wild.
"Good heavens, you needn't be so fierce! I didn't sneak
up—I just came out here to look at this *glorious* morning,
same as you!"

She proceeded to look at it, then to embrace it with a
theatrical outflinging of arms, and finally to take it over
altogether. Just how she accomplished this, Michael wasn't
sure, but he felt erased. Not erased exactly, but smudged
out, the way she smudged out unwanted lines in her char-
coal drawings—and he was bitterly resentful.

"Isn't it marvelous?" She was exulting—to herself, of
course, not to him because he was only a smudge. "Today
I can paint outside! I'll set my easel up right here, and
I'll . . ."

"No, you won't!"

Michael honestly couldn't have explained why he said it.
He didn't really want to quarrel with Lucinda—not on the
first decent day in what seemed a whole lifetime. Mainly it
was the maddening feeling of being erased, smudged out,
made to disappear. This was the story of his whole life in
Paris. In one way or another he was erased every day.
When he was sent off to the stupid school for Little
Strangers, he was erased. When he was dragged around to
all the churches and museums and art galleries and con-
certs, he was as good as erased because he wasn't really
there, he was just *along*. He was a no-person. He didn't
actually exist except in his own imagination. And now on
this really great morning when he'd managed to get all

wrapped up in something that was his own idea instead of somebody else's—even if it was nothing more than to sort of share a happy time with an old Frenchman he didn't even know and never would—his sister had to come busting in and start erasing him again. And on top of that she was going to move right in and take this balcony away from him. Well, he wasn't going to put up with it. He'd been a no-person about long enough. He was going to *un*-erase himself no matter what.

He felt himself glowering at Lucinda, who responded— unwisely, as it turned out—by assuming the haughty look that implied he wasn't important enough to get really annoyed with. "Oh, Michael," she said, "don't be a bore. Of *course* I will."

He shook his head violently. "I was here first. This is *my* place. It's—" He cast about for a slightly more solid claim than that and was newly aware of the hard, smooth surface of Old Longview clutched in his left hand. "It's my *look-out* tower." He turned his back to her, put the glass to his eye again, and pretended to sweep the horizon with it. "It's where I stand to look over this *marrr*velous city on this *glorrr*ious morning." He was mocking her tone, knowing quite well that mockery was unkind, but not caring in the least. He didn't *feel* like being kind. Besides, it took a little goading these days to get her down off her lofty pedestal or high horse.

Lucinda's trouble (and Michael had no idea how truly shrewd it was of him to have figured it out) was that she was teetering with rather frightening uncertainty on the verge of adulthood and was subject to some pretty wild gyrations as a result. One day—or one hour, or one moment—she would be more grown-up than a grandmother, and the next as much a little girl as she had ever been. The trick, as far as Michael was concerned, was to provoke her into coming down from those rarefied heights of adulthood to where he could get at her.

This time she refused to take the bait, with the result that it was Michael who found himself goaded beyond the point of no return. His mockery was disregarded, and the balcony behind him remained silent. When he couldn't stand it any longer, he lowered the telescope and looked around. Lucinda had made a picture frame with four fingers and was squinting through it toward the river and the Île de la Cité. Supposedly she was composing a landscape she would later paint. It was an arty little maneuver which Michael found unfailingly annoying because it seemed as phony as the sound of her laughter did when boys her own age were around.

"You might as well go peek through holes in your hands somewhere else," he said belligerently. "You won't be using my lookout tower."

She went on doing it. "I will," she said in a kind of singing tone. "I will—after you've toddled off to school."

"I'm not *going* to school," said Michael.

"Hah!"

"I'm not going back to that stupid school at all. Not today, not tomorrow, or *any* time."

Standing off somewhere out above the street and the balcony, Michael listened to himself make this statement. It was very impressive, very convincing. It didn't happen often, this way of suddenly finding himself outside himself, listening and watching. And when it did happen, it wasn't always impressive. Sometimes it was humiliating. He would hear himself say something so incredibly stupid that his very toes would curl with embarrassment and he would wish himself either dead or up on some mountain in

Baluchistan. But this time it wasn't like that. This was one of the good times, and he was almost frighteningly impressed with the absolute bedrock truth of what he had just said in so casual a manner. He was *not* going back ever again to the School of the Little Strangers. Not even on pain of death. Death preceded by torture.

The strange thing was that it must have sounded the same way to Lucinda, or partly so, because she halted her picture framing abruptly and really looked at him—really *saw* him for a change—and the look that came over her face was more like alarm than anything else. As if someone who ought to know had told her the sky would fall at ten o'clock sharp.

"Mike—" she began—and that proved something because she only called him Michael when she was feeling grown-up and superior. "Mike, you shouldn't—you shouldn't say things that just can't be so!"

Michael's grip tightened on the hard brass cylinder of Old Longview, which was unexplainably comforting. "I didn't," he said. Then he turned away, raising the spyglass to his eye and focusing again on Sacré Coeur, just to be doing something.

A little time passed, and in a tone that could almost have been called respectful his sister said, "Please, Mike, you don't have to prove anything. I won't tell anybody and it'll be—well—like you hadn't said anything at all."

Suddenly Michael felt quite kindly toward his sister—as a king might feel toward a subject who had seen the error of her ways. She was offering him a way out—a chance to get off the hook he had deliberately hung himself on. But what she didn't know was how terrific it felt to be unerased, to be real, to be a person. It was a dizzily satisfying feeling, and he wasn't going to let go of it. Still, he did feel kindly toward her, and a king should be charitable.

Swinging the telescope westward in the general direction of the Eiffel Tower, which after Sacré Coeur was the next highest thing in Paris, he said in a kindly-king sort of growl, without looking around, "Thanks, Cindy. But you won't need to tell anybody." He paused. (It seemed an excellent place for a pause, dramatically speaking.) "Because *I'm* going to tell them."

3

A Friendly
Monster

At the breakfast table he did tell them—after spending
the intervening time wondering in a sort of roller-coaster
fashion just how he had managed to get from where he'd
been at sunrise to wherever in the world he was now.

He had to eat a couple of extra croissants—with more
butter and apricot marmalade—in order to tell them. This
was because Dad was late getting to breakfast, and Michael
wasn't going to make his fateful announcement to anything but a full house.

Dad was late, Mom explained, because his electric shaver
had suddenly gone on strike and he was having to shave
with a razor. Proof that this was a devastating experience
reverberated from the bathroom while the rest of them

were eating—groans, mutterings, thumps, and the slamming of drawers and cabinets. He emerged at last, his face tufted with torn-off bits of Kleenex on the spots where the razor had nicked him.

"Great day in the marnin'!" Mom greeted him, imitating somebody Irish. "There must be an easier way to lose weight."

"Restrain your sympathy," he retorted, taking his seat and reaching for his coffee, all in the same movement. "Anything I can't stand it's a weeping woman."

She handed him a hot croissant, straight from the oven. "What with all that bleeding and blasphemy, have you had time to notice it's an absolutely magnificent day? Spring is here!"

"Oh, it *is,* Daddy!" put in Lucinda. "And I'm going to paint outside for the first time!" She glanced toward Michael and quickly away, adding, "I'll set up my easel over on the quayside. *Perfect* spot!"

Michael felt a surge of downright fondness for Lucinda. Sometimes she could be nicer than anybody. This was clearly an offer to abandon the balcony to him on his own terms if he would only refrain from rocking the boat. But he wasn't even tempted. It was a victory, and with victory came a heady sense of power. If he chickened out now, it would be no time at all before he'd be erased again.

All the same, it would be just as well to get it over with, on the chance that he *might* weaken. He opened his mouth, but Dad spoke first, in response to Lucinda. "Wonderful, honey! I envy you—your time—your talent—your youth—your beauty. . . ." He cocked an eye at Mom. "Be a pal, will you, and take that blasted shaver to be fixed. There's a little shop where they do that sort of thing over on the St. Honoré—just off the Place Colette. Of course, if you're busy with other things—"

"I'll take it," said Michael. No time like the present, he was thinking. Wiping his mouth carefully on his napkin, he got up from the table. "I'll take it right away."

"You dreamer!" Mom put in. "You'd never get back in time for school."

"I'm not going to school."

There it was. Rubicon crossed. Bridges ablaze. There was a long, reverberating silence. Michael got the impression, without looking at her, that Lucinda was holding her breath. Mom had started for the kitchen, bread basket in her hand, but turned back, with eyes full of question marks. Dad looked somewhat the same way, but then he finished chewing, swallowed, and smiled. "Going to take the day off, are you, Mike? Can't say I blame you. Day like this I feel like playing hooky, too. That old library's going to—"

"Not just today," Michael said in a voice amazingly firm considering the jellylike state of his insides. "*Every* day. I'm not going to that stupid school anymore."

This time the silence was virtually deafening. Through the open balcony doors came the thunk-thunk-thunk of a barge's engine on the river. Down on the street one voice called a question, and another answered. Traffic whooshed along the Quai de Montebello.

"Excuse me," said Lucinda in a strangled voice. She almost knocked her chair over getting out of there.

Mom put down on the drainboard whatever she held in her hand, came quickly back to the table, and sat down. Michael didn't look at her. He was watching Dad's long, oddly graceful fingers spread butter on a roll with careful deliberation before at last he looked up. "What have we got here—mutiny in the ranks?"

Dad spoke lightly, but he wasn't trying to be funny or sarcastic. That wasn't his way. He honestly wanted an explanation. But there wasn't one. Anyway, not one that a person could put into words that made sense. How could you tell someone that all of a sudden in the middle of a dumb hassle with your sister you just knew you couldn't stand another day in a dismal school where *nobody* wanted to be, including the people who ran it. And even if you could stand the school, you weren't going to put up any longer with being *erased* every day, turned into a no-person, shoved under a sofa cushion like a dirty sock.

Obviously you couldn't explain a thing like that, not if you tried all day. He could only shrug angrily. "All I know is I can't stand another day in that stupid school!"

"Oh, dear!"

Mom's voice sounded so distressed that he turned quickly to her, seeing nothing wrong with pushing an advantage, however small. "It's a *crummy* place, Mom. Really! I've tried to tell you, but you just—oh, *you* know."

"But it was so highly recommended! I just don't—"

"Well, it wasn't recommended by any of the kids that go there!"

"Few schools are," put in Dad. "If memory serves, you've had unkind remarks for your own school at home."

"*Dad*—it's not even the same thing!" It was hard to keep the scorn out of his voice. "This place isn't a school, it's a—a *parking lot* for kids."

"Oh, *dear!*" said Mom, more distressed than ever. "But, Mike, if you don't go to school, what *will* you do?"

An opening like that was too good to be missed, even if he knew there was scant chance it would get him anywhere. *"Go home!"* he said, nearly shouting. "Look, Mom, I know what you said last time, but I've got it figured out better now. I'll just go—"

"Mike. . . Mike. . . " Michael suddenly realized his father had been patiently repeating his name over and over. "Mike, we've talked that one to death—and I mean death. So let it rest in peace. Parents do not permit twelve-year-old boys to—"

"Thirteen," Mike interrupted.

"Thirteen-year-old boys to live alone. Or even fourteen- or *sixteen*-year-old ones—and there are at least a hundred reasons why not, all of them good ones. However. . ." He raised his voice because Michael was in the process of interrupting again. "However, you've made it amply clear how you feel about this school. We thought we were doing the right thing to send you there, but if the place is all that distasteful to you, I'm not going to force you to go there. So—"

Now it was Mom's turn to interrupt. "Well, for heaven's sake, Frank, I don't want to force him either! *I'm* not the operator of the family thumbscrews!" She paused, cocking her eyes quizzically toward Michael. "Well, honey, that brings us right back to where we've been before: Aunt Julie's."

Michael's response was a groan. Living at Aunt Julie's would be small improvement over the Little Strangers. Not that there was anything wrong with Aunt Julie and Uncle Bill; it was their horrible *twins*. The very thought of Roger and Raymond made his teeth ache. Added together, they didn't make two; they made about two thousand, every last one fiendish. Angelic on the surface; where it showed, but fiendish underneath, where it counted.

Regardless of the twins, though, he'd gain nothing by

going to Aunt Julie's because she lived in Portland, which was just close enough to Bend to torture him, but too far to do him any good. No, Portland was no good to him, what he wanted was *home*. Just the thought of it brought to mind a host of sights, smells, sounds, and tastes, any one of which was enough to deafen him to the sense, if not the sound, of what his mother was saying, blind him to the sight of her earnest, troubled face. Those thoughts of home also drove him to interrupt with the urgency of desperation. "Mom, I'd check in with the Lambertsons every day—even twice! I'd ride over there on Canuck and *show* them I was okay. And I wouldn't—"

"Mike. . . Mike!" It took even longer this time for Dad to get through to him. "Mike, I'm *sorry*. But I meant what I said. I'm afraid you have no choice but Aunt Julie's. It's—"

"No!" Treacherous tears suddenly scalded Michael's eyes, and he knuckled them angrily.

"It would be different," Dad went on, pretending not to notice, "if you didn't dislike Paris so, if you had some interest here, as the rest of us have—something absorbing to occupy you. But under the circumstances—and I hope you'll believe I'm as sorry as I can be that it had to turn out this way—the best thing—"

"Well, I *won't* go to Aunt Julie's." Michael's anger was turning on himself, which made it even worse. He'd done everything wrong, starting from his first angry word to Lucinda earlier. He snatched up the spyglass from beside his plate—for no reason except that it was there. Whirling, he fled from the room, flinging words over his shoulder as he went. "I'll *get* interested! I'll *get* absorbed! I'll get *captivated*. [One of Lucinda's favorite words.] I'll do it *right now!*"

None of these words made much sense, but they eased

his tight-wound feelings. It made even less sense to stalk
out on the balcony and there, with no more care in aiming
than a drunken gunslinger, to point Old Longview in the
direction he happened to be facing. Instantly an image
appeared, slid sideways, wobbled, then steadied, and with
a start Michael found himself face to face with a more or
less human monster with horns on its head and its tongue
sticking out. Folded wings sprouted from its back, and it
was propping its chin up with its hands as it leaned its
elbows in altogether human fashion on the corner of a flat
stone surface.

It took a moment for Michael to realize that the monster was made of stone, and another moment of peering
alongside the barrel of the telescope to be informed that
he was looking at a sculptured figure at one corner of the
great north tower of the Cathedral of Notre Dame.

He looked again through the glass. In his present
mood—or maybe it was the way the sun, well risen now,
glanced off the yellow-gray stone surfaces and softened
them—the monster that should have been hideous looked
appealing instead, even friendly. He felt, in his anger
against fate and the world, an odd kinship with this creature of stone, and he turned and shouted belligerently toward the breakfast table:

"I'm going to be interested and absorbed and captivated
by gargoyles! I'm going to be the world's greatest *gargoyle*
authority! I'm going to write *books* about them!"

At the breakfast table his parents regarded each other
ruefully. The professor thumped the table with a bony fist.
"Blast it all," he said, keeping his voice down though, "I
do feel for him. If only this job of mine were done, we'd
all head for home."

Mother patted his hand. "Well, it isn't, and we can't.

He'll simmer down after a while, and then maybe I can talk to him."

He shook his head skeptically. "We've talked it up one side and down the other already. Repeatedly."

"I know." She got up and began clearing away the rest of the breakfast things. "But don't give up. Maybe something will happen."

"Something like a miracle?"

"Who knows?" She nodded toward the light coming in the tiny window above the sink. "This is just the right kind of day for miracles. You plod on off to your grubby old library now, and leave it to me."

4

No Such Thing

Unbeknownst to anyone—least of all to Michael Horner—a miracle, or something so much like one as to make no difference, had already taken place or was in the process of doing so.

After his grandiloquent outburst he lowered Old Longview and strained his ears unbashedly toward the breakfast table. He could hear the voices but little or nothing of what was said. Probably, he told himself, they were figuring out how to bind and gag him and ship him off in a box to Aunt Julie's. By airfreight.

Soon he heard good-bye-sounding noises followed by his father's footsteps on the tile floor of the tiny hall between kitchen and living room, and he quickly raised the spyglass, pretending to be zeroed in on something over on the Right Bank. The Oriental rug swallowed any more footsteps, but various tiny sounds told him his father had come to the balcony door and was standing there, probably trying to decide whether words would be welcomed. Michael ignored him, pretending harder than ever to be absorbed in his nonexistent view. What else did a man deserve who would nail his own son up in a box and ship him over land and sea at peril of his life?

A few moments later the back of his neck informed Michael he was alone again. He lowered the telescope and simply stood there leaning on the iron railing, feeling adrift and forlorn, but unconsciously enjoying the ever warmer touch of the ascending sun.

Warming too was the thought that never again would he have to sit in the dismal classroom with all the dismal Little Strangers and listen to the dismal Mrs. Beddoes telling how deranged the major was. Not so warming, though, was the thought of the price he would have to pay for this stunning—and to tell the truth, unexpected—victory. The price, of course, was Roger and Raymond, the Unspeakable Twins. He made himself think about them for a moment, with their blond hair, blue eyes, and diabolical souls. If he knew—absolutely *knew*—that nothing would happen to prevent his having to go and live with them, he would simply get up on this railing and dive off headfirst to the street below.

Peering down at the sidewalk, his eye took in the fact that it was made of thousands of smooth round paving stones which didn't look at all inviting. Anyway there was no immediate rush. Something would turn up. Something *had* to. Lightning would strike the firing squad.

Thus flimsily reassured, Michael raised Old Longview

again. Something seemed to be jogging his elbow, telling him he'd left something up in the air—something vaguely pleasurable that he'd left undone. He concentrated. Was it the old fisherman?

It took him a while to locate his old friend of the sunrise because now there were other people down at the riverside—fishing, strolling, or just staring at the river. When he found his friend, he brought him into focus and gave a surprised snort of laughter. The old man was asleep—or anyway dozing, his chin tucked into the front of his shapeless coat. But he was still fishing. His arms were folded across his chest, one armpit hugging the pole. The wine bottle stood ready to hand on the stone parapet beside him. The white mustache fluttered rhythmically as he breathed. No doubt he was snoring.

.Asleep, though, the old fellow wasn't so interesting, and anyway, Michael soon knew that *he* wasn't the unfinished business. There was something else. . . . His head turned and he found himself staring across at the great looming bulk of the cathedral. Even at this distance—about two hundred yards or so—its solid but graceful vastness dwarfed everything around, looking ageless, as if it had been there as long as the mid-river island on which it stood. Its façade, facing due west like all cathedrals, was still in shadow at this hour, but on its south side—the side toward Michael—the buff-colored stone gleamed almost white, and the series of stone props that held up the walls and were known as flying buttresses actually did seem to soar up from the ground and bend to their mighty work with a will.

The south bell tower too—and that was what drew his eye—was awash with light, except for the closed-off interior, where he assumed a huge bell hung behind the graceful colonnades.

As he looked at the tower, Michael knew what had been jogging his memory, and in a moment Old Longview was on the job once more. He aimed at the north tower, adjusted, readjusted, and there it was again—the friendly fiend. Studying the slack-mouthed face with the lolling tongue, the big blobby nose, and enormous ears connected by a crownlike row of curly hair from which sprouted the pair of stubby horns, Michael wondered why in the world it wasn't doing a very good job because, even as he watched, a fat pigeon landed on the ledge in front on the monster and began pecking unconcernedly away. If it was supposed to frighten *people* it wasn't much good either because people couldn't see it unless they had telescopes or unless they were already up on the towers. And in either case the creature just wasn't scary, except maybe at first glance. Besides, it wasn't *trying* to look fierce; it was just leaning there on its elbows looking stupid. It looked so stupid a person felt a little sorry for it, the way you'd feel about a homely pup that wasn't as bright as its brothers. In a dim sort of way, Michael decided, this gargoyle wanted to do a good job, only somewhere along the line had forgotten what it was supposed to do and had been trying ever since to remember. Or maybe, since it had a devil's horns and an angel's wings, it was trying to make up its mind whether it should be terribly bad or terribly good. Michael sympathized, no stranger himself to this difficult decision.

This get-acquainted session with his stupid new friend was rudely interrupted as a trio of needle-nosed Mirage fighter planes came screaming over the city from the northeast. He tried frantically to catch them with the telescope but failed, and they vanished over the rooftops, the screech of their passing scrambling to catch up.

As he aimed again at the cathedral tower, he was startled when a strange monster suddenly appeared in the glass. This one, farther along the north tower's balustrade, looked very ferocious indeed. Its body was that of a muscular man, its head a weird combination of man and leopard. It hands were leopard paws with the claws showing, and it rested them on the parapet as it leaned over intently and scowlingly keeping watch on something far below.

Michael moved the glass a fraction of an inch, and there, not three feet from the leopard-man was an evil man-bird creature with an eagle beak and ape ears. It hunch-squatted horribly on the ledge, glaring down at something it obviously loathed. On a pinnacle nearby stood a winged stone angel with a trumpet to his lips and a pelican, or maybe a stork, crouched at his feet. Beyond the angel, and more interesting, was a pair of dog-monsters. They too had wings but didn't look the least bit heavenly, for while they had dog heads showing perpetual snarls and dogs' hind legs, their shoulders and arms were human.

This collection of monsters, as it turned out, was only the beginning. Moving the telescope inch by inch from pinnacle to pinnacle, corner to corner, ledge to ledge, he discovered with a sort of bemused excitement that an entire menagerie, a whole world of fascinating creatures dwelled unseen by ordinary eyes in the lofty upper levels of the ancient church. To the unaided eye they were all but invisible, blending into the structure's general design, but Old Longview brought them closer, perhaps, than they were ever meant to be.

There seemed to be every conceivable combination of bird, animal, reptile, and human shape. There was a horned devil-bird devouring a small monster who was bug-eyed with fright; a howling dog with the legs of a frog; an eagle with a dog-cat head; dragons galore; duck-eagles; a ram with a lion's tail, human hind feet and bird talons for hands; a two-headed cat-dog; a fanged monster gobbling what was either a manlike rat or a ratlike man. There was no end to them—there were scores of them, maybe even hundreds if he could count all the ones that must be on the other sides of the towers where he couldn't see them.

Lost in this weird world of the outlandish imaginings of long-dead sculptors, Michael lost track of time, of the real world, of the booby traps an unkind fate was setting up for him just around the corner. Now and then as the spyglass zeroed in on some new and splendid horror, he uttered a soft "wow" of greeting and appreciation. Every now and then he returned to the stupid friendly fiend on the north tower's inner corner.

"Hey, Charly!" he said under his breath upon one such return, thinking of a movie by that name, about an unfortunate man who wasn't very bright and couldn't spell his name properly. Charly was his favorite. Charly was a monster you could count on. He'd keep his lip buttoned and his big ears open when you had something to say. No interruptions. No wising off. Not from old Charly.

This long-distance communing with the first genuinely subhuman friend he had ever had was gently interrupted by a soft throat clearing from the doorway behind him. Mom was being tactful. He turned around, rubbing his eyes, aware for the first time that they had been operating under a strain for a long time—the left one from peering into the eyepiece, the right from being squinted shut.

Mom was dressed to go out. She was wearing a bright yellow coat and looked very springlike. Also very pretty. Her hair was the same color as his—like pencil shavings—

only on her it looked beautiful. "Sorry to intrude on the world's greatest gargoyle authority," she said, "but I've got to run. I've put things out for your lunch."

He was aware that her eyes were giving his face a thorough search while she talked. Apparently she was more pleased than displeased by what her eyes told her because she smiled in that luminous way she sometimes had and said, "Now that you're a gentleman of leisure I'll take you up on your offer. Take Dad's shaver to be fixed, will you?"

"Sure," said Michael. He felt benevolent. Maybe because she had been so tactful. Or because he didn't have to go to the Little Strangers. Or because of Charly? Because of Charly, he added, "I would be utterly delighted."

She looked a little startled by this excess of goodwill but recovered quickly. "How extremely too-too! Remember where Dad said to take it?"

"Rue St. Honoré," Michael intoned. "Just off the Place Colette. And, Mom—" A new thought had leaped on him from ambush.

"Yes?"

"Can you spare a couple of bucks—I mean about ten francs—until I get my allowance. If it won't run you short, I mean."

"*Everything* runs me short," Mom said, opening her purse. "Even the mere passing of time. Here, you can give me the change if there is any."

Partly to reward her for so nobly refraining from asking him what he wanted the money for, and partly because the idea was so new and shiny, he told her anyway. "Thought I'd get a tripod—for my spyglass."

"Oh," she said. "What are you going to do—watch a bird that just *sits* there?"

"Something like that." Michael wasn't ready—and maybe never would be—to tell anybody about Charly and his friends. The new and shiny idea was to set the telescope in a stationary position, thus leaving his hands free to draw pictures of what he saw. Charly first, then others among the monsters.

What for? Michael couldn't answer that one. He just wanted to. He wanted to ten francs worth, anyway. If he couldn't find some sort of tripod at that price, he'd find a substitute.

He found one—a tripod, not a substitute—but it took a lot longer than he had anticipated because he looked first in all the wrong places, such as camera shops where everything was too expensive, and oddment shops where there were no tripods to be found. After that he began using his head, which instructed him to go to the Samaritaine, one of the big department stores on the Right Bank. There he found a toy telescope mounted on a plastic tripod which, with the aid of a little friction tape, would do quite nicely. The telescope itself he presented, speaking a mixture of French and sign language, to the first small boy he met. *"C'est pour toi, mon enfant!"* (It's for you, my child), he declared magnificently, thrusting the toy into the hands of the urchin, whose expression was a comical blend of distrust and greed.

The grandiloquent words, however, brought a glint of humor to the boy's dark eyes and he bobbed his head in a suggestion of a bow. *"Je vous remercie, Père Noel."*

Thus formally thanked, Father Christmas marched on down the Rue de Rivoli to the Rue du Pont Neuf, across the Seine on the Pont Neuf to the Quai des Grands Augustins, along that quay until it became the Quai St. Michel, and along *that* to the Quai de Montebello, and there he was home—mission completed, though a good deal later than he had thought to be.

The apartment, however, was still gratifyingly untenanted, and he lost no time in introducing Old Longview to its new pedestal. But when he sighted in on the corner of the tower where Charly lived, he got an unpleasant shock. Charly and his friends had company—human company. A group of tourists were milling around behind the stone parapet on which Charly leaned. They were aiming cameras in all directions, pointing, gesticulating, and jabbering away in no telling how many languages, and Michael found them excessively annoying. Somehow he hadn't expected to find plain old dull *people* up there—and what right had they anyway to intrude into this private world of his?

Thinking about that, he had to admit it was silly. Yet that was the way a telescope made you feel—as if whatever appeared in the little circle at the end of the brass tube belonged to you personally. The instrument caused everything else—above, below, beyond, and on all sides—to vanish utterly, leaving only what remained within the magic circle. And it all belonged to you, like a toy you could hold in your two hands.

These noisy strangers (he didn't actually need to *hear* them to know what a racket they were making) were unlawful trespassers in this little universe he held in the hollow of his hand. He toyed pleasurably with the thought of reaching out a godlike thumb and forefinger, plucking them one by one from behind the parapet, and flipping them a couple of hundred feet into the Seine.

He was distracted from this cozy daydream when one of the trespassers, a young man with a great deal of hair and very little chin, leaned on the parapet beside Charly, sticking his tongue out and imitating the gargoyle's pose while the young woman with him took a photograph. Beside the man, Michael decided, Charly looked quite intelligent and downright handsome. He also looked much bigger than the man. All the other trespassers laughed fit to split, and Michael decided that instead of flipping them into the river, he would just hold them over the edge and drop them. Splat. Splat. Splat.

All that saved them from this messy form of execution was the banging of the apartment door and Mom's voice calling, "Mike! Are you home?" She sent him down to the street to lug up a box of groceries. Right after that Dad came home, then Lucinda, and after that things didn't really quiet down until after dinner.

When he got back to the telescope at last, Charly was waiting. Michael wondered in a shivery sort of way just how long Charly had been up there keeping his endless vigil above the city. A lifetime—no, a whole string of lifetimes, probably. Come to think of it, Charly did look as if the rain and the wind, the heat and the cold, had rounded any edges he might once have had. Maybe though, the softening of his contours was just a trick of the light, which was fading swiftly now that the sun was down.

Michael moved the glass in a quick survey of Charly's neighbors. The evil ones didn't look quite so evil, the devourers not quite so mercilessly voracious, the devourees just a shade less terrified. (After all, another day was passing, and they hadn't been eaten yet.) It was on the whole as peaceful and contented a set of monsters as was likely to be found anywhere, now that all the tourists were gone and time for sleep was coming.

"Good night, monsters." Michael formed the words with his tongue and throat without actually speaking them. "Pleasant nightmares."

He had actually taken the eyepiece from his eye during the infinitesimal instant it took for the eye to flash to his brain the message that something was there that he hadn't seen before—something unbelievably strange, something it was impossible to believe could really exist. In his haste to get the glass quickly back into position he jammed a knuckle into his eye, which promptly swam with fluid impossible to see through. Exclaiming with annoyance, he squinted, blinked repeatedly, and finally snatched the handkerchief from his pocket and wiped the offending eye. Then he lifted the glass again, spent another few seconds locating the proper corner of the tower, and peered intently, holding his breath to steady his aim.

There was Charly. There was the rapidly darkening parapet. There were the ghostly figures of the other monsters. And that was all.

He wiped both eyes and carefully looked again. Same story.

Why then did his brain keep telling him—actually insisting—that in that vanished instant his eye had glimpsed a new gargoyle, a different gargoyle, a very tiny gargoyle? Not only that (so said his brain, the silly thing), it was a *pretty* gargoyle.

Holding Old Longview with both hands, he scowled at it accusingly. Maybe it was lying to him—as likely an explanation as any. Whatever the explanation, though, he knew one thing for absolutely certain sure:

There was no such thing, in this world or out of it—as a pretty gargoyle!

5

Performance
by a Bird

For a person accustomed to sleeping like a long-en-
tombed mummy, it was a restless night. In the first place it
took Michael at least ten minutes to get to sleep, a lifetime record, and in the second place he kept either waking
up or dreaming he was waking up, each time in a sort of
panic for fear the sun had risen and he had lost his first,
last, and only chance of the day to catch another glimpse
of the world's prettiest gargoyle.

The result of all this nighttime turmoil was that when
the day did come, he had settled down to some real
mummy-style slumbering, and the first thing he was aware
of was Mom sliding the drapes aside and the dammed-up
sunshine bursting in.

He came off the couch as if it had been a trampoline, landing in the middle of the floor and reaching for his pants, which were draped over the back of a chair.

"Fire drill?" Mom inquired interestedly, a question he chose to ignore as he writhed his way into his clothes. Breakfast slowed him down, though, because there were eggs and British bacon. These were now-and-then treats because they were so expensive, and in the Horner household money was in chronically short supply. Dad's favorite homemade joke was that "professors' pants all come with built-in poverty pockets."

In one way it was a lucky thing he had overslept because it meant the others were nearly ready to go their assorted ways and Michael didn't have long to wait before he was left in sole possession. Mom was the last to leave, and at the door she lingered a bit, looking at him in a half-worried way. "What," she asked hesitantly, "will you do all day long, Mike?"

Hah! He was ready for that one. No fool he. "Research," he replied with what he hoped was an air of competence. No nonsense—strictly business. The word sounded so impressive that he said it over to himself. Research. A highly respected word in the family because that was what Dad was doing, along with most other people who taught in colleges.

"In what—uh—field?" Mom inquired.

"I already told you. Gargoyles."

She watched his face, but when he didn't laugh or smile, she made a quick little sighing sound, smiled herself, and went out, softly closing the door.

Michael felt mean, but not mean enough to need to do anything about it. Then he hurried out to the balcony.

Starting with Charly, whom he greeted with a cheerful,

though whispered "Hi," he examined all the monsters he had seen the day before, plus some he hadn't, and all the spaces in between. Nowhere was there a gargoyle whom even its mother could have thought pretty.

Putting Old Longview aside to give his eyes a rest, he uttered a disgusted noise. Never had he been so completely baffled. The only explanation for the whole thing was that he had seen something that wasn't there. A hallucination. Or a combination of his own imagination with something fleetingly glimpsed in failing light. And yet. . . .

He parked the spyglass on the chair and stalked off to his sister's room where he brazenly borrowed one of her books of drawing paper and a pencil to go with it. The only way to get the imaginary gargoyle out of his mind was to get busy on the real ones.

It worked. Once the telescope was mounted on its tripod and Charly's imbecilic countenance centered inside the magic circle, Michael sat with the drawing book in his lap, his head near the eyepiece so that he could glance easily from Charly to the drawing that soon began to take shape.

Like Lucinda, Michael had been born with a talent for drawing—inherited, everybody said, from Mom's father, who had been an artist and illustrator. Unlike Lucinda, though, Michael had no burning ambition to do anything in particular with this talent. He used it only to amuse himself when there wasn't anything better to do.

But in the case of Charly it was different. He really wanted to do right by Charly. No reason, he just did. And the other monsters as well, when he could get around to them.

Slowly, because he was taking great pains, the winged monster took shape on the paper. Michael erased frequently, altered a bit of line or shading, chewed his tongue, squinted and unsquinted, and in the process mercifully forgot about the pretty gargoyle who didn't exist. He also, like a true artist, forgot about the time until all at once he became conscious that he had been thirsty for a long while. Propping the drawing against the chair back, he went to the kitchen for a sody-pop. (Thanks to Dad, who had borrowed the term from his grandfather, all soft drinks were known to the Horners as sody-pop.) Bringing it back, he stood looking down critically at his work. There was something he hadn't got right—something about the angle of the hand that propped up Charly's chin. He took a swig of his drink, sat down again, and peered through the glass.

Blast and double blast—there were the tourists again! Anyway, *some* tourists. This bunch had a guide—a large woman wearing an orange scarf over an untidy mass of hair, also orange. She did all the pointing and most of the talking while the others listened through their mouths.

Michael tried to ignore them, but it was hard to do because there seemed to be more of them all the time, all crowding into the magic circle. Charly ignored them, staring with his customary lovable stupidity in Michael's general direction. The tourists were gathering in a knot in the middle of the open space between the two towers while Orange Hair waited for the stragglers. At last they were all assembled. No—wait—there was still one more. A small straggler with—

Zoinnnng! Electrical vibrations ricocheted around inside Michael's head, and he nearly pushed the tripod overboard as he snatched the glass and aimed it.

There, smack in the middle of the magic circle and very much alive, stood the prettiest gargoyle in the world!

It wasn't a gargoyle, of course; it was a girl. But she *was* pretty. Michael felt like screeching for pure joy. Yahhh—hooo! Not because it was a girl. And pretty. And about his own age. But because she proved that his brain was in pretty good shape after all. No hallucinations. No loose rivets. It was an enormous relief.

The good-shaped brain, however, didn't permit him to enjoy all that relief for more than a moment or so because it started right in on a whole new set of questions. They went like this:

So okay, it's a girl, not a gargoyle. But what's she doing up on that tower at eleven o'clock this morning with a bunch of strangers when she was there at seven or so last night all by herself?

What do you mean, strangers? Because they're strangers to you doesn't mean they're strangers to her.

But they are!

How do you know?

Because she's French.

How do you know *that?*

Shrug. I just do. She *looks* French.

Well, even if she is, what's that got to do with it?

Plenty. Because they're *not* French.

How do you know *that?*

Because they're not *talking* French.

How do you—

Because they don't stick their lips out and sort of hunch their shoulders the way you have to do when you talk French. And anyway, French people wouldn't be running around sight-seeing in their own city on a working day.

Okay, genius, if you've got an answer for everything, why *is* she up there this morning when she was up there last night? Has she been there all the time? Does she *live* there?

Don't be silly. Nobody *lives* there.

The Hunchback of Notre Dame did.

He was fictitious, stupid. This girl is real!

Well, *I* know she's real—you think I'm blind?

This mental bringle-brangle might have gone on the rest of the day, getting farther and farther away from anywhere, if the prettiest gargoyle hadn't suddenly discovered something to stand on up there behind the stone parapet and proceeded to stand on it, making more of herself visible. Then, leaning her elbows on the top, about the way Charly was doing, she suddenly turned her head and looked straight down the middle of the brass tube that was Old Longview, smack into Michael Horner's eye. He almost ducked.

It was an extremely odd and unsettling experience. Like peering through a keyhole and meeting another eye. And even while his good-shaped brain was yelling at him that it was an absolute physical impossibility for her to be actually *seeing* him, he went on thinking up stupid Charly-ish apologies all full of duh-duhs and doltish guffaws because she'd caught him staring at her.

Even while all this was going on—thanks to the amazing ability of the brain to do all sorts of things at the same time and at lightning speed—Michael was busy taking note of the surprising fact that maybe this girl really wasn't pretty after all. But on the other hand, there was something that made you want to go on looking at her.

She had nearly-black hair and big dark eyes, but right there the prettiness ended. You wouldn't call her bony, but the bones of her face were more in evidence than they ought to be in someone really pretty, and her mouth was sort of wide. It turned down at the corners, but instead of looking sad, as downturning is supposed to, it looked as if she were about to laugh. Her brows were darker than her hair, and instead of curving like half-moons, they lay mostly straight, tilting upward and outward like a pair of wedges lying on their sides. The whole effect was a kind of eagerly expectant one, as if she were holding her breath waiting for the fireworks to go off.

All these observations took about as much time as a deep breath, and then she stopped staring him straight in the telescope and did something that made him gasp as if he'd been whacked in the stomach. Grasping the outer edge of the parapet, which looked about two feet wide, she gave a fast wriggle-hunch and was suddenly lying right on top of it, with her head sticking over the edge, no telling how many feet above the courtyard in front of the cathedral. She appeared to be studying something or someone down there.

Michael's innards went swoop-lurch, and various muscles went through the motions of shoving her back off the parapet. The imaginary exertion left him actually a little breathless. To his relief it turned out that his innards were not the only ones affected, for suddenly a man—one of the tourists—came bursting into the magic circle with out-stretched arms and scooped the prettiest gargoyle from her dizzy perch. He set her down behind the parapet and pro-ceeded to deliver the sort of lecture Dutch uncles are fa-mous for. Maybe he *was* Dutch, for all Michael knew, but he certainly wasn't her uncle because he wasn't speaking her language. It was easy to tell he was speaking mainly sign language because he kept shaking his head violently, slapping the top of the parapet, pointing dramatically downward, waving his arms, and turning red in the face.

As for the girl, she watched him solemnly, eyes very

wide, to all appearances vastly impressed, yet all the while giving Michael that breath-holding, waiting-for-the-fireworks feeling. After a time the man stopped talking and stood looking down at her severely. At that point a brilliant smile illuminated her face, and she reached out and patted the man on the arm. It was a sort of motherly gesture, as if she were comforting him. Then she peered skyward, pointing, reversed the pointing finger, and tapped her own chest with it. She spoke: *"Je suis oiseau, moi!"*

For a split second Michael was convinced he had actually heard her speak. Instead, he had read her lips, thanks to her expressive gestures and the fact that it was impossible to say the word *oiseau* followed by *moi* without making three distinctive and unmistakably French lip puckerings. She had told the man she was a bird. And now, in case he was left with any doubt of her meaning, she spread her arms wide (she was wearing a sweater of tanager red) and with smooth foot action invisible to Michael swooped around in a full circle in front of the man before soaring away with gentle, graceful motions of her wings to disappear into whatever never-never land she had flown from.

Michael felt himself grinning in appreciation of a first-rate comic performance. Then he noticed that some of the man's companions were grinning too. One was calling something to him in what was obviously a jeering tone, to which the man replied with a rueful grimace and a gesture which clearly stated he would henceforward permit the young of the unpredictable French to fall from whatever cathedral towers they chose.

For his part, Michael brought the curtain down on the entire performance by the simple expedient of lowering the spyglass. Until that moment he had been unaware that his arms ached fiercely with the effort of holding it steady for so long a time, while his eyes, now relieved of their strain, felt permanently crossed. Not only that, he was starving.

Before going in to eat his lunch, he studied the uncompleted drawing for a moment. Somehow the gargoyle looked more friendly than ever, though no smarter, and Michael felt odd and altogether unreasonable stirrings of excitement. "Hey, Charly," he said, using his silent-speaking muscles, "what are you getting me into?"

That he was being got into something was beyond question. It was a feeling he had in his bones, which he had seldom known to be mistaken.

Very reliable, those bones.

6

Encounter on
a Tower

About twenty minutes later the reliable bones were
carrying Michael down the three flights of stairs to Butchery Street and up its short length to Little Bridge Place
(which Lucinda and everyone else insisted on calling the
Place du Petit Pont). There he hesitated under a plum-
colored awning of the café of the same name, contemplat-
ing topping off his lunch with a tasty *glace vanille*. When
you ordered a *glace vanille*, you got a dish of ice cream
with a big fan-shaped wafer that somehow managed to
taste good even while tasting a little bit like cardboard. He
also contemplated the financial realities, which were that
his pockets contained exactly three francs and sixty
centimes. This would have covered the price of the ice

cream, but he had a shrewd notion that there would be a fee for climbing to the towers of Notre Dame. There was always a fee.

Stoutheartedly doing without ice cream then, he crossed the Petit Pont from the Left Bank to the Île de la Cité—that battleship-shaped island in the Seine which had been in ancient times all there was to the city of Paris. Two or three minutes later he arrived, along with dozens of other people, on the sidewalk directly in front of the great vaulted central portal of the cathedral. He stood for a few moments, tilting his head up toward the towers and the colonnade between them. By this time the sun was far enough past noon that it was shining obliquely on the massive expanse of the façade. (Anybody who'd ever been around Lucinda and didn't know that the front of a cathedral was its façade just wasn't listening.) Its color was that of warm beach sand, and all its arches and colonnades and carved stone figures coaxed the eye to move ever upward until the blue of the sky showed empty and clean between the soaring square towers. Michael could make out the figures of the gargoyles protruding over the stone ledges, but here, almost directly underneath, it was impossible to tell which was which, and still less possible to see clearly any of the smaller, human figures moving about up there.

All around him people milled and laughed and chattered in a Babel of tongues. His ear, an expert by this time, heard French, of course, and German, British-English, American-English, and harsh, throat-clearing sounds of Dutch, the singsong of Swedish or perhaps Danish, and the Oriental languages, which, even to an ear as good as his, were indistinguishable. It occurred to him that if he were to be blindfolded and led around the streets of Paris, he would always know when some great monument or museum or ruined antiquity was nearby, for those were the places where the foreigners gathered.

As he thought the word "foreigners," the wooden door at the left-hand side of the main portal burst open, and a file of boys marched out of the cathedral, led by a tall, harassed-looking young man with fair hair and long toothy face, who couldn't have been anything but a British schoolmaster.

As if just to prove Michael right, this individual turned to his chattering charges, held both arms commandingly aloft, and addressed them in a refined sort of shout. "All right, chaps! Right around the corner for the staircase to the tower. Follow me!"

The boys, some about Michael's age, others older, dutifully straggled along behind their leader, and Michael, deciding on the spur of the moment that he had nothing to lose, straggled too. They marched around the corner to the north side of the cathedral, through an open iron gate, and up a few steps to a door at the base of the column-shaped stone buttress that rose up toward the tower above. Here the group came to a bunchy halt while the teacher bought tickets. When the line began to move, Michael moved with it, passing in a moment the little glassed-in cubicle in which sat the inevitable woman ticket seller. She said nothing to him, so he, not being one to push himself forward, said nothing to her. A quick glance as he passed showed him that the price of admission was two francs—about thirty-six cents.

A penny saved, he told himself virtuously, is two centimes earned. Benjamin Franklin would have been proud of him.

The stone stairway began spiraling upward, around and

around inside the buttress, and Michael spiraled with it. The steps, pointed at the inner ends, broad at the outer, like thin wedges of pie, were so worn by the scraping and stamping of thousands upon thousands of feet through the endless years that they looked as if they had been scooped out in the middle by a giant spoon. This made for uncertain footing, and Michael soon learned that the price of inattention was a stumble. The light, too, was tricky, coming as it did from an occasional dim overhead bulb and a still more occasional slit of an embrasure in the wall, which looked to be about four feet thick.

Pausing at one such embrasure to peer through it toward the rooftops below was what made him lose count of the steps somewhere in the eighties. When he guessed he had climbed about a hundred steps, he came to a side stair, off to the right. He could see that it led into a large room which had paintings on the walls and a counter at which a woman was selling color slides and booklets. His British companions were led into the room, and there he parted company with them, continuing up the stairs which, after another hundred steps or so, narrowed to not much more than half their previous width. At this point he caught up with voices he had been hearing from above. They belonged to a middle-aged couple who had paused to catch their breath. Seeing Michael, they smiled and pressed their backs against the wall to let him pass. The man said something to him in German. Michael smiled too, shook his head to indicate ignorance of their language, panted loudly to show that he too found the long climb strenuous, and went on doggedly moving upward.

Just as he was beginning to wonder if the end of the stairs would ever come, it did; he stepped out into a new and brilliant world—and almost the first thing he saw was Charly!

The "almost" part of it was that in the first instant his eyes were overwhelmed by the vastness of the city stretching out below, the sun flooding it all with light and picking out the moving spots of color that were cars, boats on the Seine, and people. After that first glimpse he turned his head to the right, for no particular reason, and there, mere feet away, was Charly himself with his tongue lolling out, leaning on his corner of the parapet and looking either very patient or very bored but really too stupid to care.

Michael threw a quick glance at a group of people standing farther along the parapet, then turned with what felt like a silly grin and said under his breath, "Hey, Charly, it's me—Mike!"

Charly said nothing, just went on steadily staring off to the southwest. That was Charly all over—strictly business, no goofing off. Mentally commending his stony friend on his devotion to duty, and assuring him that he'd be seeing him around, Michael turned his attention to the rest of his surroundings. That, after all, was what he'd come all the way up here for, wasn't it—to look around?

Charly's perch was on a corner of a stone balcony at a front corner of the north bell tower. The railing he leaned on zigzagged its way clear around the tower, and all around the south tower too. Behind the railing was a walkway, but right at Charly's back it was blocked by a heavy iron grille, so the tourists were confined to the walkway along the front of the tower. This was a disappointment to anybody who might want to look at the gargoyles on the other sides.

But since there was nothing he could do about it, Michael, like everyone else, moved southward along the parapet. Stopping halfway along the front of the north tower, he peered up at the two archways rising to its top. Behind these, obviously, were the bells, closed off from

the weather by a great black metal casing. Next, he looked
back toward the doorway through which he had just
stepped and had to grin at the sign which stood propped
there, forbidding descent of the stairway in three languages, the least comprehensible of which was the English:

> Descente Interdite
> Taking Down to Forbid
> Absteig Verboten

Next he turned and leaned against the railing to look
down at the pavement he had trod so short a time ago. His
stomach did a fast sink-swoop. The people down there
looked like heads with legs flopping around under them.
Cars, like beetles with invisible legs, moved in a counter-
clockwise direction around the sides of the huge open
space that stretched from the cathedral's façade to the
front of the Prefecture of Police, a vast, low building about
a hundred yards to the west. This open space was known
(courtesy of Lucinda) as the Parvis de Notre Dame. Parvis
in turn (courtesy of Major Beddoes) was an old form of
the word "paradise."

Just to give himself another taste of the sink-swoop feeling, Michael inched a little farther over the ledge and
looked a little straighter down, wondering just how much
of a drop it really was.

"You are now standing approximately one hundred and
fifty feet above street level," said an obliging voice about a
yard from his ear. It was the schoolmaster, and in another
moment Michael was surrounded, trapped, a prisoner of
the British. The voice went on: "As you doubtless have
already observed, you are now in the presence of the
famed gargoyles of Notre Dame." Except for the accent it
could have been Michael's father.

"Actually"—it sounded like "*ek*-chlih"—"these creatures are not gargoyles, they are chimeras [ky-meeras]. Gargoyles—quite lit'rally *gurgles*, or *gargles*—are downspouts shaped like beasts through whose open mouths the water runs off the roofs. Look 'round and you'll see them everywhere. All the old Gothic structures have them. *However*—" The schoolmaster cleared his throat resoundingly, to round up some straying attention. "However, since the chimeras are all but universally known as gargoyles we shan't be stuffy about it. We shall call them gargoyles too." He followed this with a remark in Latin which must have been genuinely funny because a yip of laughter greeted it, leaving Michael feeling left out of the fun and pretty ignorant besides.

"These gargoyles, as we shall call them," the schoolmaster went on, "were put up here not much more than a hundred years ago by the architect Viollet-le-Duc. They replaced earlier ones which had long since succumbed to the elements or to vandals. Now you may wonder. . . ."

The lecture went on. It was interesting, and Michael would actually (*ek*-chlih) have liked to hear more, but restlessness was troubling him—an unfinished-business sort of feeling—and he squirmed through the knot of boys with the aid of elbows and apologetic mutterings. Breaking free, he moved along to the tower's south corner, where the balustrade jogged outward in another little balcony such as the one presided over by Charly. At its outer corner stood Charly's opposite number, a monster with a billy-goat beard, horsy ears, and a broken-off horn. A pretty ferocious sort of monster, not at all the sort, like Charly, that a person could take his shoes off with and settle down and be comfortable.

Michael hurried a little as he passed behind this gargoyle and its companions because the balcony, sticking out from the façade, gave him another attack of sink-swoop. After that he found himself in the broad open area between the towers. Here he was on a level with the steeply sloping metal-sheathed roof of the cathedral proper, and it was easy to see that the huge building was in the form of a cross extending to the east. Soaring upward from the point at which the two sections of the roof met to form the cross was a spire made of metal and so ornately fashioned that it looked like lacework. Up and up and up it rose, higher than the tops of the great stone towers between which Michael stood.

Now, of course, he could see the inner sides of both towers and found them alive with still more gargoyles. There were devils and devourers, humans and near humans, and shivery brooding bird-beasts. There was even a quite realistic elephant, who looked patient and wise and just a little tired.

Michael let his eyes rove quickly over them all, making mental notes to have a longer look some other time. Right now. . . . Well, right now *what?* Well—why beat around the bush about it? —he was looking for a hint, a trace, a glimpse, an echo, of the only pretty gargoyle in the world.

Why? Well, to satisfy his curiosity. And anyway, why *not?*

Look, stupid, "why not" is no kind of answer to "why." But let it go and answer this one: Suppose you find her—what happens then?

I find out how come she's up here all the time, that's what.

You mean you just walk up to her and say in French, "Hey, you, how come you're up here all the time?"

Well— Oh, leave me alone. How do I know what I'm going to—

Fortunately this profitless argument was brought to an end by a sound. Even before it succeeded in distracting him, he had subconsciously taken note of a sound which was so much a part of Paris by this time that he often hardly noticed it. It was the rapid-fire hee-haw, hee-haw of a police or emergency vehicle. The sound was approaching swiftly, and in a moment he caught sight of a flashing blue light as the vehicle—one of those box-shaped blue police vans—came streaking across the Pont St. Michel to disappear at its island end, blocked from view by the Prefecture but appearing again seconds later to go skittering around the edge of the Parvis and then to swing sharply left to disappear through a portal of the Hôtel Dieu, the main central hospital of Paris, which stood at right angles to Notre Dame on its right.

During this entire process, now that he thought about it, a policeman had appeared at every single corner, as if he had sprung right out of the pavement, to control the traffic while the emergency car passed. The police of Paris, it had occurred to him before, seemed to have everything very well under control. Looking down now, he counted at least a dozen, or maybe twenty, in their blue uniforms with the round, military-style hats trimmed with red. They strolled along, often in pairs but sometimes singly, watching, watching everything without really appearing to do so. He wondered vaguely if there were always that many *flics*, which was French for cops, around Notre Dame, but then he supposed there were. It was a busy place, with so many tourists and all.

He was about to turn away from the scene below him when another vehicle with a blue light on its top slid to a halt in front of the left-hand portal below. This one was not a van, but a long, sleek car. Its light was not flashing, nor was its hee-haw sounding. As it stopped, a uniformed officer stepped up to it, leaned down to peer inside, then saluted briskly and stepped back again. The car door opened, and a man in a dark suit and hat got out. He said something to the uniformed man, then reached back toward the car. An arm appeared, handing him an object which Michael recognized after a moment as a camera in a case. The man then took off his hat to slip the camera's strap over his head. Because Michael was directly above he saw that the man's head was bald except for a circle of graying red hair. Then the hat was replaced, and the man nodded toward the car, which slid away from the curb and quickly disappeared from view. Immediately thereafter the man with the camera also disappeared, crossing the sidewalk toward the cathedral entrance.

Michael stepped back from the railing, wondering about what he had just seen—not with any great urgency because it was of no concern of his, but wondering all the same. The policeman had saluted, so the other man must have been somebody important. Some kind of police official? A high-up detective?

Abandoning this useless speculation, Michael glanced across the river toward home. There it was—top floor but one on the corner of the white plaster building whose front windows looked out on the Rue de la Bucherie and its side ones on the Rue St. Julien-le-Pauvre (Poor Julian Street, to Michael) and the tiny park known as the Square de René Viviani. Just beyond the trees in the little park, now turning yellow-green with new leaves, rose the red tiled roof of the ancient church of St. Julien le Pauvre. It was small wonder, he thought, that Old Longview had brought Charly seemingly within touching distance. Now, even with just his unaided eye he could make out some of the iron curlicues on the railing around the Horner family's tiny balcony. If he'd brought the telescope with him, he could practically read his own fingerprints on its surfaces.

He wished he *had* brought it with him—not to read fingerprints—but because from up here he could see almost everything there was to be seen in every direction. But it didn't matter; the point now wasn't sight-seeing; the point was to—

He turned his back on the great panorama and looked carefully at everything and everybody close by. The people were no help. There wasn't a pretty gargoyle among them, with or without a tanager-colored sweater. There was none among the true gargoyles either, crouching or leaning in profusion as they did along the parapet on either side of him and along the inner sides of the two towers. He moved over along the inner face of the south tower, passing behind one of the devouring monsters. There between the stone colonnades he saw a door in the metal sheathing that housed the bells, and above it a sign: BOURDON GALERIE. This, of course, meant the room, or platform, where the bourdon was, and a bourdon, under the circumstances, could scarcely be anything but a bell—a *big* bell, more than likely. A smaller sign at eye level informed him that one must apply to the *gardien*—the keeper, or watchman—in order to visit the *galerie*.

Michael would just as soon have had a look at the bell, but there was no *gardien* in sight and the door was locked, so he backtracked to the parapet, negotiated another outthrust balcony at the north corner of the south tower, and proceeded along to the south corner, where there was another balcony, this one blocked by another iron grille. There was no way, then, to get to the parapet on the south side of the south tower unless—

Unless. . . Michael's innards did a small but definite
swoop. Unless you really wanted to! It would be no trick
at all for somebody his size or smaller to climb up on the
railing and squeeze between the squawking-bird gargoyle
squatting there and the iron grillwork. Once around that
you could probably follow the parapet and its balconies
clear around two sides of the tower, the south and east,
before running into the grille around there by the bell
gallery door. And on either of those two sides nobody
visiting the towers could see you. *Nobody* could see you—
except somebody in a helicopter or. . . or somebody over
on the Left Bank with a telescope!

Was that it? Had Old Longview been aimed at the
parapet on the south side when he caught that first split-
second glimpse of the prettiest gargoyle? Was she around
there this minute—the almost-pretty girl with the waiting-
for-the-fireworks face?

Michael eyed the squatting stone bird. It would be so
easy to climb up, straddle its back, and squeeze past the
sharp-pointed horizontal bars of the grille. So easy—but
impossible. People were all over the balustrade behind him,
jabbering away as usual. They'd see him climb over and
make a big thing of it. Scream for the *gardien*, who was
sure to be around somewhere.

And anyway, he told himself, the chances were a million
to one there would be anybody around there but pigeons.
He had been jumping to wild conclusions, and not for the
first time. He could jump to more conclusions in five
minutes than most people could in a week. A real mental
athlete. Mike Horner—boy genius.

As crushed by this sarcasm as might be expected, he
promptly decided to go on up to the top of the south
tower to find out what could be seen from up there. The

doorway was right there in front of him and people were straggling through it, some taking the stairway down, heading for ground level, others starting up to the pinnacle of the tower.

This ascent was much more difficult than the ascent of the north tower because the stairs here were wide enough only for one person, yet the traffic was moving in both directions, making it necessary for everyone to squeeze past everyone else. The climb seemed to take forever, but at last he emerged a little breathless through an arched doorway in a little round tower topped by a conical roof like a stone duncecap. Here it seemed to be truly the top of the world. Nothing impeded the view here, and Paris stretched out endlessly in all directions, full of splendors seen and splendors imagined. If he had stopped to think about it he might have recalled the words of his father, spoken so short a time ago: "Give Paris half a chance and she'll get to you."

At the moment, though, he was too preoccupied to recall anybody's words. He soon discovered by leaning as far as he dared over the square-topped stone railing that the balustrade directly below could not be seen. By looking across at the north tower, which was identical with this one, he could see that this railing was recessed behind the face of the tower on all four sides, as if the top of the tower had beveled edges. To see anybody on the parapet below, a person would have to be a true gargoyle, like some he could see on the opposite tower with their necks thrust far out, mouths open to let the water gush out.

Up here the tower's top was covered by a low-pitched, six-sided expanse of weather-darkened metal. There was a young man up at its apex now, aiming a camera off toward the north, where Sacré Coeur gleamed a brilliant white in the afternoon sun. Michael walked around three sides of the railing to stand looking down from the inner corner on the west. Here he could see below him a part of the balustrade extending between the towers. There were people down there, of course, and he felt rather superior to them, as most people do when viewing their fellow creatures from above.

As on the day before, a dumb-looking young man was posing in front of Charly while his girlfriend took his picture. Stupid man. Stupid girl. Poor Charly.

Just a few feet away from the stupid man, another man took off his hat to scratch his head and with that simple act captured the total and undeviating attention of the boy who stood looking down at him from the south tower high above. The head had a slightly sunburned bald center surrounded by reddish hair going gray. It was the man from the police car.

While Michael watched, hypnotized, the man replaced the hat, turned his big body slowly toward the south tower, and just as slowly tilted back his head until Michael found himself staring down into the coldest, bluest, hardest, most relentlessly piercing and probing pair of eyes he had seen in all his life.

Though the air was as warm as a blessing, a shiver ran up his back.

7

Warning to
a Bird

The longer Michael stared into the face of the man below him, the more he felt like a daisy having its petals pulled off. He loathes me he loathes me not. . . .

It wasn't an evil face—not at all—but it was a face as cold and unfeeling as the stones of the cathedral. The eyes, deepset under brows of red going gray, could just as well have been agates for all the warmth they showed. They looked as if they had never missed anything and never forgotten anything—and of one thing Michael was absolutely sure: If this man ever saw him again, he would remember him.

In a moment the man lowered his unsettling gaze and moved along the parapet where he was no longer visible

from above. Michael's feeling of relief was instantly interrupted by a surge of panic. What if the man came up here
to the top of the tower? This brought on another idiotic
argument, Michael against Michael.

Well, what if he *does* come up here? *You* haven't done
anything!

I came up here without paying my two francs, didn't I?

Look, stupid, the city of Paris isn't going to send a
high-powered police detective up here to—

But anyway, all I have to do is get down out of here
and—

And meet him on those stairs? Stomach to stomach?

So it went, until reason prevailed, as it usually did
sooner or later. As reason put it, the detective (if he *was* a
detective) couldn't possibly be after Michael. (He probably
looked at everybody in that spine-chilling way, just to
keep in practice.) Whatever he was doing had been arranged long before Michael showed up at Notre Dame.
Otherwise no ride in a police car. No getting saluted at.
And no camera. The camera—Michael was particularly
proud of this brilliant stroke of logic—was the detective's
disguise. It made him look like a tourist. No Parisian—least
of all a policeman—ever went around with a camera hanging on him.

So what *was* he up here for? Well, Michael didn't know,
of course, but he had a very strong suspicion that it had
something to do with the prettiest gargoyle. After all, if
Michael was looking for her, other people could be looking
for her too.

And speaking of looking for her—her certainly wasn't
accomplishing anything just standing around up here
thinking. Up here there was no possible place for anyone
to hide, whereas—

The inspiration struck him like a jolt of electricity, and he bounced. He bounced away from the railing and dashed for the tower and the stairs. Oh, brilliant, brainy Michael Horner! With any luck. . . .

With a little more luck than he really deserved, he told himself a couple of minutes later, he found the British delegation bunched around the little door to the bell gallery while a man in a blue uniform and very thick glasses unlocked the door with one of the keys on a large, jangling ring. He was talking over his shoulder, warning that his little tour would be conducted entirely in French. Michael, short of breath after his dash down to the base of the tower, stifled his puffing as best he could and sidled up to the fringe of the group, trying to look like one of Her Britannic Majesty's more absentminded subjects. Nobody paid any attention to him, and in a moment he filed through the door with the others.

In contrast with the bright light outside, the gloom in here was deep, but soon the surroundings became clearer as his eyes adjusted. The hush of awe that had closed over the boys was broken by an exclamation in imitation Cockney. "Crikey! Wot a ruddy great barn loft!"

The others laughed, but with the restraint imposed by this awesome place. Michael saw what the boy meant about a barn loft, though this was far more vast than any barn. What first struck the eye was the contrast with the outside, where everything was made of stone. In here everything was made of wood. On all sides rose vast time-blackened beams hand-hewn from whole tree trunks. These were interlaced with a maze of crossbeams and braces held in place by huge bolts, cables, and massive wrought-iron plates.

At the left a wooden stairway led upward, its handrails

gleaming in the dim light, oiled and polished by thousands upon thousands of hands. Pushing his way through the knot of boys, the guide started up these stairs. *"Suivez-moi!"* he commanded, and everyone, including the schoolmaster, obediently followed.

At the head of the staircase the guide halted and pointed dramatically. *"Voilà! Le grand bourdon de Notre Dame!"*

The dramatics were justified, Michael decided as he peered around the head of the boy in front of him. The great bell loomed massively above the wooden platform on which everyone stood, a giant among bells, dwarfing everything. The guide's speech speeded up, and Michael began missing words and whole phrases, but he got the gist of it. The bell weighed fifteen thousand kilograms. It was electrically operated now, like the smaller bells in the north tower, but in earlier days it had required the efforts of eight men dragging on ropes to toll it. It was rung only on religious holidays and special occasions.

More information followed; then the guide ducked under the lip of the bell, which hung about five feet off the platform, and motioned for the others to crowd in with him. There were about twenty boys, Michael guessed, but there was room and to spare for all of them as they clustered around the huge clapper, which probably weighed more than all of them put together. He gave himself the shivers, thinking what it would be like if something gave way and the monstrous thing dropped down over them, a vast bronze prison cell. And then, if somebody were to start pounding on the bell.... He jumped when the guide tapped its edge with a little wand he carried and a clear note sounded, conveying just an infinitesimal hint of the thunderous peal the giant was capable of.

After that the guide shooed the group out from under the bell and went on with his monologue, leaving Michael free at last to get on with the job he had come to do. The job was to use his eyes—and the rest of his head as well.

He had already observed that another stairway led upward from this platform, and now he let his eye follow it. It was hard to tell just where it led, so deep was the gloom high above. But somewhere up there amid the network of beams there must be another platform, used no doubt when it was necessary to make repairs on the bell's suspension mechanism. It would be a perfect place to hide, he thought, provided a person didn't mind being locked in the tower until the guide brought the next party of sight-seers.

He squinted, straining his eyes to pierce the murk, half expecting a flash of movement, a hint of color—that bright scarlet sweater. . . .

There was nothing, peer and squint as he might. He tried to ease his sharp disappointment by telling himself scornfully—and correctly—that if the girl was hiding up there, it wasn't likely she'd move or show herself just because *he* was looking for her. After all, other people had eyes, and they might be searching, too. He glanced at the guide, confirming his earlier observation that the man wore extremely thick glasses. That was comforting; at least *he* wouldn't be likely to spot her.

Not comforting at all, however, was the thought that immediately followed: The whole thing was a wild-goose chase; he'd let his imagination run away with him, as usual; there was really no convincing reason to think the girl was anywhere near here simply because he had seen her twice before. By this time she could be anyplace—safe at home, for example, and if he had any sense, he'd go home too.

Having got that settled all logical and shipshape, Michael was in a state of thorough unreadiness for what happened next.

What happened next was a sneeze. It was a small, delicate, restrained sort of sneeze. It came from the upper regions, and it came smack in the middle of what was undoubtedly the *only* moment of silence inside the bell tower for the last ten minutes. The guide had just finished a sentence, and nobody happened to be shuffling his feet or muttering to his neighbor. It was, for all practical effects, a little gem of a sneeze.

Fortunately, of all the two men and twenty-odd boys gathered there on the bell platform only one had been thinking in terms of small girls in the upper reaches of bell towers, and that one took action with a speed he found incredibly dazzling when he got around to thinking about it later.

Michael had never particularly prided himself on the swiftness of his reflexes, but no one could beat the speed with which he now whipped the handkerchief from his pocket and sneezed a counterfeit sneeze into it. It was even a quite delicate and girlish sneeze, and he followed it instantly with another, just a little louder and less delicate, and a third that wasn't delicate by any standard. He then topped off the entire performance with enough snuffling and snozzling into the handkerchief to drown out any further noises that might be coming from on high, eyeing his rather startled fellow tourists in an apologetic manner.

Now the shuffling and muttering had resumed, and the guide was speaking again and waving his arms to herd the group back down the stairs. This abrupt end of the tour caught Michael unprepared. He tried to hang back, having already taken note of the fact that it would be simple enough to duck behind one of the beams and let the party go on without him, but the general movement toward the stairway carried him along, and the chance was lost.

And anyway did he really want to? Well, yes, he did, but would it be the smart thing to do? Maybe the girl wouldn't want to explain herself to him or talk to him at all. Her reasons for hiding were her own business, after all, and he'd only be butting in. He'd feel pretty silly— wouldn't he—sitting around up here talking to himself while he waited for the guide to come back with another group—*if* he came back. For all Michael knew, there would be no more bell tower visits today, and there he'd be, locked up for the night. The very thought of the turmoil in the Horner household if that happened was enough to keep him from doing anything rash. No, there was nothing for it but to go on out with the others.

But wait—the detective! In his mind he was peering once more into those stone-cold eyes. What else could he possibly be doing up here but looking for the girl? And she was hiding—no doubt about that. But why? A young girl like that couldn't be a criminal. . . .

Now his brain was going at jet speed, though it wasn't giving him any sound answers. All he knew for sure was that he was on her side. If she didn't want to be found—by the law or anyone else—then he didn't want her to be found either, and it was his job to help her. And to help her right now meant warning her that the law was after her. She couldn't know it; otherwise, she wouldn't have been doing her bird act for a bunch of tourists. But *how* could he warn her? There was no way—and no time!

This, it seemed, was Inspiration Day inside the skull of

Michael Horner. The British contingent was bunched at the door, which the guide was holding open as they filed out. He had already received from the schoolmaster's hand a reward for his services and was jingling his keys a little impatiently while he waited for the last of the boys to pass.

Suddenly one of those boys dropped to one knee to tie a shoelace. Actually he merely fiddled with it, stalling while the rest made their way around him and out the door.

"Allez! Allez!" urged the guide irritably, whereupon the shoelace fiddler rose quickly, turned his back to the door, and addressed the upper reaches of the tower in tones which themselves rang like a bell.

"Mam'selle oiseau—prenez garde! L'aigle est tout proche!"

Thus was Miss Bird warned, through cupped hands, to beware that the eagle was nearby. (Michael would rather have said "hawk" but didn't know the French. Naturally he couldn't come right out and say "police.") The cupping of the hands was in the hope the guide might not be able to make out exactly what he said.

In case he had, though, Michael turned and started out under the gaping official's nose, with an expression of imbecility that rivaled Charly's. "The birds, m'sieu," he said confidingly, still in French, "I always talk to the birds."

This time his own words brought on another inspiration, and while the guide's eye bulged further, he whirled once more to face the tower's interior. *"Je suis Michel—l'ami des oiseaux. Je reviendra!"*

Thus Michael, the friend of the birds, promised that he would return, then marched out into the shadow of the tower, where he made a hideous face at the first gargoyle he saw. Filled with admiration for his own performance, he found it hard to keep from flapping his wings in a bird act of his own. *Clever* Michael Horner!

8

Wanted:
By Police

Clever Michael's high regard for himself lasted about as long as it took him to spiral down the south tower's stairway, cross the Pont Double, walk up the Quai de Montebello to the Rue St. Julien-le-Pauvre, and climb three of the four flights of stairs to the apartment.

At that point he uttered an exclamation of disgust, turned around, and went straight down again. He had forgotten he was supposed to go back to the repair shop over on the Right Bank and pick up his father's shaver.

Enroute he turned the proper corners, crossed the proper bridges, and walked along the proper streets, all with mechanical efficiency, but his mind kept prowling around the towers of Notre Dame. It also kept nagging at him, asking what he had done that he shouldn't, what he should have done that he hadn't, what he ought to do next, and what in the name of good sense was the prettiest gargoyle up to anyway—and who *was* she?

It helped a little to sum up what he did know, which wasn't much. He knew she was hiding up there in that unlikely place. He knew she had been up there for at least two nights, and no telling how many more. He knew (or almost knew) that the police were looking for her. And he knew that, at least until he yelled his crazy warning at her, she hadn't considered herself in much danger of being found. Maybe she still didn't. Maybe—and small wonder—his warning hadn't meant anything to her. "Miss Bird, the eagle is near." It sounded pretty stupid, now that he thought of it. But what else could he have said, with the guide right there and. . . .

His step faltered, and he came close to whacking himself in the forehead, French style, with the heel of his hand. What a lame-brain! How *numb* of him not to think of it till now! —Why hadn't he tried repeating his warning in *English?* Lots of European kids knew all kinds of languages, and maybe this girl knew English. The guide didn't, so Michael could have yelled anything at all. Well, no point in hashing it all over now. But next time. . . He continued on his way, not even considering that, just possibly, there might not *be* a next time.

On his way back, carrying the shaver, he found himself hurrying a little and taking a slightly longer route in order to cross the island on the Rue de la Cité where he could look across the Parvis to the front of the cathedral. Its stones absorbed the rays of the sinking sun, turning to a soft yellow-gold. At the moment, though, Michael had no eye for beauty. He scanned the now-familiar abode of the gargoyles for human figures. There were a few, but none of them the right one.

Momentarily he contemplated a quick dash up those formidable stairs for a quick look around, but it was almost five o'clock, the time the tower would be closed. And anyway, what good would it do?

He dawdled disconsolately on over the Petit Pont, hurried across the busy Quai de Montebello when both the traffic light and the policeman at the intersection told him to, then dawdled some more in front of the café on the corner. He was vaguely dissatisfied with himself and vaguely reluctant to join his family and have to start thinking about other things. Cars and motorbikes hummed and roared along the street; pedestrians hurried by, many pausing at the little green box of a newsstand where an old woman was dispensing copies of *France-Soir* and *Paris-Presse*. One of each was on display in a rack at the side of the box. Michael's eyes had been staring for some time at the black type before he focused on it.

PEUR D'ENLEVEMENT, said the headline in *France-Soir*.

Fear of lifting up? That didn't make much sense. He looked at the other paper.

VICTIME D'UN KIDNAPPEUR? asked *Paris-Presse*. Well, that was clear enough. One of those American words adopted by the French. So somebody was feared to be the victim of a kidnapper. All this headline reading reminded him of Dad. The professor was always intending to buy a paper on his way home and almost always forgot to do it, so that he had to go out after dinner and get one. Michael could win some points by bringing one home.

He stepped up to the counter where the papers lay

folded, fishing in his pocket for a franc. Then he froze—turned to stone, ice, wood, iron, whatever. From the printed page under the black type stared the face of the prettiest gargoyle!

He was never sure later whether he had paid his franc to the woman or just grabbed a paper and dashed along Butchery Street to the little park, where he sat down on the first stone bench he came to. At any rate, whether he bought the paper or stole it, there he sat, stretching his mind all out of shape to understand as much as he possibly could of what was written about the mysterious disappearance of thirteen-year-old Danielle de la Tour from the sumptuous residence of her uncle on the Île St. Louis. The uncle, described as a "well-known industrialist," feared she might have been kidnapped, though nobody yet had demanded money for her return.

The police, it said, had nothing to say about the possibility of kidnapping but had given the girl's photograph to the press and would welcome information from any citizen concerning her whereabouts.

There was a lot more, and Michael struggled through it as best he could, missing perhaps half of it. At last he lowered the paper to his knees, let his gaze drift across the Seine to the spires and buttresses of the great cathedral, and with something like awe concentrated on the thought that of all the millions of people in the city of Paris there was only one—Michael Horner, of Bend, Oregon, U.S.A.—who knew where Danielle de la Tour was to be found.

Danielle of the Tower. The name was almost too appropriate to be believed. Unless her name had influenced her choice of a hiding place. His eye wandered on up to the south tower. Already it seemed hard to believe it was only a matter of hours since he had been up there. And surely it must have been days and days since he had put Old Longview in place on the little tripod—

France-Soir made papery flapping noises as he leaped to his feet, charged across the street, and assaulted the stairway to the apartment. What set him off like a rocket was the recollection that the telescope must still be standing there like a huge pointing finger, and practically *anybody* could be looking through it.

And sure enough, somebody was.

As he burst through the tiny hallway into the living room, the first thing he saw was Lucinda sitting in *his* chair behind the balcony railing, holding *his* drawing in her lap and peering through *his* telescope, and looking, for all he knew, straight at the world of the magic circle. Oh, double blast her anyway!

Furious words boiled around in his mind, crowding to find a way out. Fortunately, the only way out was jammed at the moment with gasps for breath. It was fortunate because, suddenly aware of his tumultuous arrival, Lucinda turned, with one of those rare, luminous smiles that were so much like Mom's, and held up his drawing of Charly. "Oh, *Mike*," she exclaimed, "this is *good!*"

There went the wind out of Michael's sails, every breath of it. There was no question that she meant exactly what she said, and also it seemed obvious she hadn't seen anything through the telescope except maybe Charly. So his angry outburst died, and as he caught his breath he felt himself grin foolishly and heard himself reply with one-hundred percent false modesty, "Oh, it's just a dumb old drawing." As he spoke, he peered at it with a fresh eye and found it a rather impressive piece of work.

Properly ignoring all this modesty, Lucinda went on. "It's your *line*, Michael—you have such a strong *line!*"

This was the arty sort of talk that ordinarily annoyed him immensely, but this time it didn't seem to strike him that way. "And what a great idea—gargoyles! I just took a little peek through your telescope. . . . Marvelous!"

She was getting artier by the second. Probably just couldn't help it, he thought with unwonted charity. Anyway, the flow of arty talk made it easier for him to sidle in front of her and remove the spyglass from the tripod as unobtrusively as he could manage, twisting the focusing ring at the same time. Apparently no harm had been done this time, but he resolved that from now on, wherever he went, Old Longview would go too.

Lucinda was working herself up to a real attack of elder sisterliness, telling him how he really owed it to himself to develop his artistic talent, as she was developing hers. No telling how far she might have gone with the lecture if Mom hadn't provided a diversion. Michael had been aware that she had come through the hall from the kitchen and paused, waiting for a break in Lucinda's monologue. Now she joined them, giving his shoulder a quick squeeze. "Cindy's right, Mike," she said. "You've done a first-rate job with old what's-his-name—your gargoyle friend."

Michael felt the warm little glow that a compliment from Mom always gave him, and he threw a quick smile at her. "Charly," he said. "I call him Charly. Without the *e.*"

"Hey, that's good!" Mom said. "Maybe you really *are* going to be an expert on gargoyles."

Always quick to seize an advantage, he said, "I *told* you I was. Only they're not gargoyles at all."

"They're not?" said Mom.

"Then what are they?" demanded Lucinda.

Knowledge was going to Michael's head. "Chimeras," he said.

"Ky-*meeras?*" put in Lucinda suspiciously. "How do

you spell it?" She didn't take kindly to displays of superior knowledge on his part.

Michael was cornered. He had no idea how to spell it.
But the sun had not set on Inspiration Day. "*En français
—chimère*," he quoted loftily, and before she could ask
him how to spell *that*, he hurried on to explain what a
gargoyle really was.

When he had finished, Mom sighed exaggeratedly. "You
sound just like your father," she said.

Lucinda was still suspicious. "How come you know so
much about it?"

It was a temptation to explain, but instinctive caution
told him to play things close to his chest. The time might
come when the less known about his movements, the
better. "Oh, I looked it up," he said carelessly and put Old
Longview to his eye in the hope of more or less politely
calling a halt to this cross-examination.

It worked in part. Mom went back to the kitchen, and
Lucinda stopped asking questions—but she didn't go away.
Michael swung the telescope toward the cathedral tower,
blurry images moving with their usual swooping swiftness.
After a minute Lucinda said, "*I* thought it was pretty
decent of me not to land on you for helping yourself to
my sketchbook." She was still sitting with the sketchbook
open to his drawing, and now she closed it. "Don't *you*
think it was pretty decent of me?"

She waited a moment for a reply, and when there was
none, she looked up angrily. "Well, *don't* you?"

When there was still no answer, she glared at his motion-
less, oddly rigid figure. His face was getting red because he
had been holding his breath for quite a while without
knowing it. "Mike-*ull!*" she burst out, tried beyond her
patience now. "I'm *talking* to you!"

Startled, he jumped. Her last words were actually the

first he had been conscious of. For all this long, hypnotic moment he had been staring straight into the magic circle that now framed the face of the prettiest gargoyle. And she, for the second time in as many days, was staring right back at him. And not only that—

"Michael—what's the *matter* with you? Why are—" There was a sudden change in her tone. "What are you looking at? What do you *see* over there?"

That did it. Suddenly all too aware of what was going on, he nearly dropped the spyglass in his hurry to snatch it from his eye, then made everything worse by thrusting it behind his back.

"Mike, you're *hiding* something!" Lucinda was triumphantly accusatory. "What have you been *doing?*"

He was mercifully spared the necessity of answering by the appearance of Dad, arriving home from his day of research and study. "Hi Dad!" he whooped, with a lot more enthusiasm than the moment really called for.

"He's up to something, Daddy!" announced Lucinda, a great believer in striking while the iron was even lukewarm. "He's been doing something he shouldn't!"

Dad put his book bag down on the couch that was Michael's bed and regarded his son mildly. "That right, Mike?" he said.

"Of course not!" Purity of conscience rang in his tone.

"Oh, yes, it is, Daddy—and you'd better find out about it!"

"I expect I will," replied Dad, sitting down on the couch and stretching his long legs out, "the minute the police come after him."

Michael cringed, even though he knew his father wasn't serious. The police were a little too much on his mind as it was.

"Oh, very well!" said Lucinda, turning herself into a super-grown-up. "Don't say I didn't warn you! " She swept from the room, leaving father and son face to face. Father winked. Son grinned. It was one of life's better moments. Then Michael turned quickly back to the balcony and the business at hand.

The business at hand, so frustratingly interrupted, was the last vision he had seen in the middle of the magic circle: the oddly humorous, pretty-unpretty face of Danielle de la Tour, the prettiest gargoyle and probably number one on the most-wanted list of the Paris police. In the vision the face was seen only from the nose up as the girl who was feared kidnapped leaned on the south balustrade of the south tower of Notre Dame de Paris looking straight at Michael Horner, so it seemed, and playing on a large harmonica.

9

Rendezvous with a Gargoyle

The next day dawned silkily warm and bright, the very dream of spring, and Michael Horner dawned right along with it, rumpled and ill used by the night but crammed to the ears with the spirit of do or die.

If there had ever been a longer night since creation's first day, he didn't want to hear about it. Maybe he hadn't tossed very much, but he had certainly *turned* incessantly, and the lumps in his couch had multiplied like mice. But determination burned like a pure flame within him and went right on burning even while he padded over the cold tiles of the kitchen floor and held his head under the tap in the sink. Come what might, the sun would not set that day without his having come face to face with the prettiest gargoyle and learned from her own lips what kind of game she was playing.

Toweling his head and face vigorously, he tried not to think how far away ten o'clock was—the time the towers would be open to the public. At least, he thought, searching for a bright side to look at, he didn't have to spend all those hours squirming around in bed. There were preparations to make, family routines to endure, and in spite of the long night a lot of thinking still to do.

The thinking had mainly to do, of course, with Her. (In his mind he had taken to calling the prettiest gargoyle Her. It didn't seem natural to use her name without any sort of introduction.) It had taken a lot of thinking the night before to figure out what She was doing over there behind her private balustrade. Because of dinner and the comings and goings of his family, he had been able to snatch only brief glimpses with the spyglass and then put two and two together as best he could. It had been rather like watching television, with the sound turned off, while pretending not to, and at the same time carrying on a conversation with a room full of people.

At any rate, following the harmonica performance— which she appeared to enjoy immensely—she had disappeared behind the parapet, then popped up again a moment later with what he identified after some difficulty as a tiny transistor radio. This she placed on the stone ledge, propped her chin on her folded arms next to it, and listened. He was able to watch long enough to see the expression on her volatile face alter completely at least four times: from indifference to skeptical questioning, to utter delight to profound annoyance. During the last stage she stuck out her tongue at the radio and made an impudent face at which Michael found himself grinning.

The next time he could look she was holding the radio aloft and dancing to its music, twirling and gliding from one end of her lofty promenade to the other. Only her head appeared above the parapet, the rest of her showing a bit fuzzily through the ornamental fretwork below the railing.

The last thing of all that he had been able to see was the hardest to figure out. She had gone to the eastern corner of the tower, where the walkway stuck out in one of its little balconies, and had done her disappearing-reappearing act again. At first it looked as if she were doing some sort of calisthenics. Her head bobbed up and down, and so did her hands, which were holding something floppy. Not until she had ducked for the last time and put in no further appearance did the explanation dawn on him: She had lain down. The floppy thing was a blanket or a sleeping bag. Unlike the rest of the gargoyles, who were doomed to stand guard all night, the prettiest one was going to get some sleep.

One result of this performance was that Michael, for the first time in his life, found himself lost in admiration for a girl. In the first place she had far more courage than any girl he had ever known—and maybe more than most boys. Could he himself, he wondered, lie calmly down to sleep on a ledge high up on a great cold stone cathedral, surrounded by hideous monsters and securely locked away from the rest of mankind by heavy wooden doors a hundred and fifty feet below?

Then he had to admire her planning abilities. She must have reconnoitered like a general preparing for battle—finding all the hiding places and how to reach them, no doubt learning a lot of things Michael hadn't even guessed at. And the sleeping bag, the radio, and no telling how many other refinements. Plus food and drink, of which she must have only a limited supply. (But Michael had plans about that.)

Perhaps most of all, he had to admire her choice of a place to hide. Because Notre Dame was the biggest, most prominent thing in sight; swarming with people by day and locked up tight at night, it seemed the last place anyone would look for a missing person. The very fact that he alone of all the millions in Paris had spotted her—and only by the strangest of coincidences at that—proved that when it came to hiding, this amazing girl belonged in a class by herself.

There was plenty of room for admiration all right, but still there were one or two details that weren't very smart of her at all, and he had every intention of telling her so as soon as he had made her acquaintance. One was that scarlet sweater. It showed against the yellow-gray stone like a signal flare. Then there was the bird act of the other day. It wasn't very smart to call attention to herself like that, even if it was to a bunch of foreigners. Unless she *wanted* to be found, which didn't seem at all likely in view of all her other precautions. And anyway *he* didn't want her to be found—certainly not until he'd had a chance to find out what it was all about.

All these reflections occupied him no longer than it took to get into his clothes, and that was scarcely any time at all. Then, hugely admiring his *own* forethought and efficiency, he got right to work on the first of his preparations.

He began a new gargoyle drawing. His purpose was to make as much progress on it as possible before it was time to go haunt the cathedral. That way, if he didn't get back to the drawing and somebody asked him later what he had been doing all day, he could just show it to them. If that person drew an incorrect conclusion, that was hardly his fault. A quick look with Old Longview gave no indication that She had risen with the dawn, as he had. And since everyone who is up early always feels superior to everyone who isn't, he was able to turn to his task in a glow of virtue. His choice of subject this time was an eerie, hooded, brooding sort of monster not identifiable as human, animal, reptile, or bird. All but its face was enveloped in the folds of a sort of nun's coif that covered all its body but the feet, which looked more reptilian than bird-like.

Strangely, under the circumstances, Michael soon became so absorbed with his drawing that he forgot everything else, including the excitement of the day that lay ahead. When at last he heard getting-up sounds from the other rooms, he was startled to find that more than an hour had passed. Even while hurrying to put the drawing away so he could claim to have done it later, he paused for a moment to wonder how this could be so. Never before had he worked at drawing anything with such concentration. What was going on anyway—with him and these crazy gargoyles?

Giving up on that question, he took a hard look at another: Why weren't Dad and Mom as concerned about him as they had been—about not going to school and all that? He had thought fleetingly about it last night, but now the problem returned. They seemed altogether too relaxed about him, and once, now that he thought about it, he'd seen them exchange conspiratorial glances after looking at him. Was something going on he didn't know about?

That question went unanswered, too, and was forgotten

in its turn as one by one the family went their several ways and he was free at last to make his final preparations.

First he put on his lightweight windbreaker, which was a sort of undistinguished tan-gray. At the moment he needed its pockets, and later it would become the temporary property of the prettiest gargoyle—to cover up that crazy red sweater.

Next, from the more or less secret compartment of his suitcase in the hall closet he got out his reserve money supply and counted it, even though he had an accurate idea of how much was there. (Ever since he had learned what money was good for, he had been a firm believer in putting some by for emergencies.) Just as he had thought, the total was thirty francs—about five and a half dollars. Not bad. After a moment's calculation he replaced about half of it. The rest should be plenty, and the rule was never to clean out his reserve. Thrifty, provident, farsighted, praiseworthy Michael Horner!

In the kitchen he found and appropriated a small flashlight. After checking it (it worked) he put it in a pocket of the jacket. Next—string. A thorough search finally turned up a full roll of heavy brown twine which no doubt belonged to the professor of archaeology. It too went into a pocket, along with a sort of mental receipt which promised its eventual return. Into other pockets went a pad of scratch paper, a pencil, a large iron nut, a tiny French-English dictionary, a remnant of a roll of Scotch tape, and the story of the *victime d'un kidnappeur* which he had clipped from last night's paper.

His next maneuver was to sit down with a sheet of paper and print the letter *M* repeatedly in graduated sizes from about four inches high down to less than an inch. Taking this odd creation out onto the little balcony, he fastened it with tape to the wall of the building just to the right of the balcony.

The final operation was to make two cheese sandwiches with mayonnaise and two peanut butter and jelly sandwiches, wrapping them with waxed paper, as his mother always did, and putting them into the lunch box which he had always carried (in some remote previous incarnation) to the School of the Little Strangers. This left room for two bottles of sody-pop and a small handful of stuffed olives.

Now it was half past nine and time to go. He stood in the middle of the living room for a time, trying to think of things left undone. Then he picked up the lunch box, tucked Old Longview under his arm, and set forth to pay a visit to the prettiest gargoyle of Notre Dame. After so much highly intelligent thought and meticulous preparation, nothing—he felt in his reliable bones—could go wrong.

Things began almost immediately to go right. He was halfway across the Pont Double when he became aware that there was something familiar about a man who was walking along the sidewalk ahead of him. He wore a blue uniform, shiny with wear, and something about him jingled, not like coins, but like—

Keys! That was it. And he wore—as Michael could see when the man turned his head to one side—a pair of very thick glasses. It was the guide to the bell gallery, the *gardien* of the towers. He was probably on his way to work.

With the instinct of the born skuldugger Michael slowed his pace to stay behind. After the previous day's performance there was no point in attracting any further notice to himself. Nearsighted the man might be, but he wasn't altogether blind. Besides, who knew what advantage might be gained by keeping him in sight?

Who indeed? About forty seconds farther along, the guard turned to the right at the very foot of the cathedral, walked the few paces to the stair landing from which all visitors emerged at the end of their long descent from the south tower, and disappeared from Michael's view. His keys jangled louder, though, and Michael, himself soundless on rubber soles, hovered just out of sight, listening.

The sounds told their story: key fitted to lock, lock clicking, door creaking open, catch being fastened to hold it, shoes scraping on stone, then solid tread proceeding upward. *Gardien* on his way to another day's work. After a moment Michael followed. Boy on his way to adventure without having to pay two francs to get there.

If there were such things as shadowing schools for student detectives, Michael reflected as he climbed, the kindergarten course would take place on a stone spiral stairway. So tight were the turns that the shadower had only to keep quiet, stay about a dozen steps behind, and keep his ears open. The shadowee remained in ignorance that he was not alone. When the footsteps above him halted, as they did two or three times while the man rested, Michael halted too, poised for action in the unlikely event that the man should start down again.

He didn't, and at last the sounds informed Michael that his subject had reached the top and was crossing toward the north tower, where he had his little office.

Michael stole up the last few steps but remained inside the stairwell for what he judged to be a full minute to allow the man plenty of time to get out of sight. While waiting, he speculated whether the guide would now have to go all the way down the north tower stairs to open the door there and then toil back up again. It seemed unlikely. Probably somebody else—the ticket seller, maybe—would open that door when ten o'clock arrived.

Speculation over, waiting period over, Michael took a deep breath and stepped out where the vast sunlit panoply of Paris once more lay before him. But he wasted no time admiring it, swinging quickly to his left to face the gargoyle-guarded corner balcony blocked off by the heavy iron grille. Never would he have a better chance.

It was the work of only a moment to shove the lunchbox and Old Longview between the bars and set them on the other side, then to pull himself by one of the horizontal bars to the top of the parapet and squeeze behind the screeching bird, being careful not to look straight down, and drop to the walkway behind the grille. Then, retrieving lunch box and telescope, he slithered on around that balcony, which faced west, then the next balcony, which faced the river and the Quai de Montebello.

A moment later he stepped around the final angle to the walkway that ran along the south side of the tower, and there, on a rolled-up sleeping bag, her back against the wall of the bell tower, brown arms hugging blue-clad knees and dark head cocked birdlike toward him, sat the prettiest gargoyle.

"*Holà*, Michel—friend of birds!" she exclaimed in a tone of pure delight. "What has kept you so long?"

10

Hungry Fiend

What she actually said was: "*Vous êtes arrivé à la fin des fins*" (You have come at the end of ends), but Michael got the idea plainly enough and found it impossible not to grin, seeing the lurking laughter in her eyes, while he struggled to frame a suitable reply. As usual, he found that speaking a language not his own presented both a disadvantage and an advantage. On the one hand it made communicating one's real thoughts difficult, if not impossible, but on the other hand it made saying anything at all seem a linguistic triumph.

What he came up with was, "Maybe *you* can fly up here, but I've got to wait till they open the door—and *walk* up."

He might as well have spared himself the effort because

she wasn't listening. Her eyes had fastened suddenly on Old Longview, and comprehension was spreading over her face like a fast-motion dawn in Technicolor. A second later she was on her feet without, apparently, having exerted any effort and firing off an excited barrage of French so fast that he didn't catch a word. He shrugged elaborately to convey incomprehension. *"Parlez lentement!"* he commanded.

But to speak slowly was apparently more effort for this fizz-water girl than she could tolerate, and before he could even blink, she had plucked the spyglass from his grasp and was peering through it toward something imaginary high in the sky above Montparnasse to the south. *"Je suis Michel* [I am Michael]*"* she informed him. Then, still before he could move or speak, she thrust the telescope back at him, whirled, and performed her bird-in-flight routine in a figure eight that ended where it began—right in front of him. "Mam'selle Oiseau!" she proclaimed triumphantly.

Michael nodded emphatically to show he understood, then frowned and pointed at the scarlet sweater. It would be a good idea, he was thinking, to get it straight right off the bat that Michael Horner was a person who really thought things through and could be counted on to assert masculine leadership. "That sweater," he said, "it—" What he wanted to say was "sticks out like a sore thumb," but hadn't a clue how to go about it. He shifted his approach. "It's too. . . too. . . *visible*." He produced the word like a magician producing a rabbit, and she nodded with smiling approval, rather in the manner of a teacher whose dullest pupil has managed to spell "cat."

The suspicion grew in him that he was being teased, which was unfair, considering all the trouble he'd gone to on her behalf, not to mention the further trouble he was quite prepared to go to. "I *know* I don't speak French very well," he said with considerable heat. "Why should I? I'm not a—"

"*Mais tu parle bien—très bien! Sans accent!*"

This outburst jerked the rug straight out from under him. When a French person told a foreigner he spoke French without accent, it was about the highest praise he could think of, according to Dad, who should know. And her face was so serious he had to believe she meant it.

He was wondering if the proper thing was to say thank you when she added, *"Tu es anglais?"*

"No, not English, I—"

"Canadien?"

"No—American."

"Ah!"

He stared, on the defensive again—something about the way she spoke that single syllable. "What do you mean— 'Ah'?"

"Rien. Rien du tout!" Nothing at all. As she spoke, she flung both arms out and let them fall helplessly, with a look of injured innocence so convincing that Michael felt like apologizing.

Apologizing for what? He'd better get a grip on himself. Having anything to do with this girl, apparently, was like riding a roller coaster—exhilarating but wearing. Accordingly, he squared his shoulders and said, rather more loudly than necessary, *"Alors!"* A word which has about as many uses in French as "okay" has in English, *alors* in this instance meant "All right, let's cut out the monkey business and get down to brass tacks." He pointed to the sleeping bag and added firmly, "Sit down."

To his happy surprise she obeyed promptly, clasped her knees again, and looked up at him with eyes so filled with trust and submissiveness that he looked back at her with deep suspicion. But the fact of her sitting when he told her to gave him a sort of momentum, and he launched into the speech he had been rehearsing, off and on, ever since the night before.

"I've told you my name. Now I'll tell you my home is in Oregon, but right now I'm living in Paris—just over there on the Left Bank. I discovered you with my telescope, and I have come to help you. Yesterday I was only curious about you, but then I discovered there was a policeman—a policeman without uniform." He hadn't been able to find the French for plainclothesman. "I thought he must be searching for you, so I tried to warn you. Then I. . . "

There was quite a bit more to the speech, but the rest of it was never spoken. He had a feeling, even while he was struggling with the words and phrases, that it would turn out that way, for almost at once the prettiest gargoyle had begun to show signs of internal bubbling, then of boiling over. Her eyes grew wider and wider, and she began to nod faster and faster, the dark, straight hair with its hint of a wave bobbing furiously. At last, she burst out, "You did warn me—so very cleverly, and I thought—"

Michael waved his arms and made shushing noises. "Wait—I'm not finished—" But it was like trying to stuff the steam back into the teakettle, and he gave up, contenting himself with imploring her at intervals to slow down.

"I thought, 'This boy who looks so kind, so good, he is my *friend*. He will help me escape from those who would torment me and make of my life a misery.' And you promised you would return, so I knew you would do so. And now you *have* done so and I will rest content. Oh, Michel, you cannot know how magnificent it is to find a friend in this huge city that is without a heart. So I will tell you."

Michael managed to interject a "Please slow down" at this point, but nothing more.

"My home is in the south, in—in Avignon, whence I have fled sorrowing and fearful. My name is Celestine Dumenjou, and I am the oldest of eleven children. My parents are very poor, sometimes there is no food on the table. They weep . . . they pray . . . 'What shall we do!' . . . they cry! So I cannot find it in my heart to blame them for selling me!" Here she paused significantly, wiped from one eye with a dainty knuckle what Michael could have sworn was a real tear, and waited for a reaction from her audience.

"*Selling* you?" inquired the obliging audience.

Her long lashes lowered like tiny theater curtains, and her voice took on an artistic quaver. "Truly. They affianced me. To a very rich and ugly man who is himself old enough to be my father. In two years' time I was to marry him. So I ran away to Paris and have hidden, as you see. But now—now"—she cast fearful glances in all directions, as if the gargoyles might be detectives in disguise—"now my—my fiancé has sent these evil men to— What are you doing?"

This last was delivered in a suspicious tone that didn't at all match what had gone before and was occasioned by the activities of the audience, who had stolidly begun to remove an assortment of objects from the pockets of his jacket. A large ball of twine appeared, followed by a small pad of paper, and a little blue book with *Français-Anglais* in silver letters on its cover.

Michael laid these objects on the stone slab before her, like offerings to a small but lively idol, and then brought out still another—a clipping from a newspaper—which he placed solemnly in her hand. "A little something to read . . . Celestine," he said. Then he stepped back, watching as she unfolded the clipping, waiting for her gasp of dismay and embarrassment. The prevaricator exposed.

He should have known better, he was telling himself a moment later. Even on so short an acquaintance he should have known better. She gasped all right, but not with dismay. It was a gasp of pure outrage. *"Oh! This frightful photograph!"* The French—*"Cette photo effroyable!"*—sounded even more outraged than the English. *"It makes me to look like this!"* She crossed her eyes alarmingly, sucked her lower lip under her upper front teeth, elevated her wedge-shaped eyebrows to impossible angles, and uttered an explosive "Pouah!" which obviously was French for "Ugh."

"Oh, brother!" said the grinning Michael. "That's a *girl* for you!"

She turned the silly face into a frown and shook her head impatiently. "Silence, if you please, while I read."

"Okay, *Madame la Duchesse!*" said Michael with top-heavy irony, and sat down beside her, leaning back against the metal sheathing of the bell chamber. Almost at once he was conscious of a faint aroma that came from her. Not perfumy, like the stuff Lucinda slathered herself with after a bath. Just, well, just girl smell. Hard to pin down, but on the whole interesting. Like puppy smell.

Silence, it quickly appeared, was a one-sided affair. The prettiest gargoyle turned out to be about the noisiest reader he could imagine. She punctuated her perusal with "Hos," "Has," and other interjections expressive of an entire alphabet of emotions. Sometimes she merely muttered darkly like an apprentice witch composing a spell to cast. Once she loosed a trill of delighted laughter that seemed to run all the way up the scale and disappear into the musical stratosphere.

Michael found himself wishing she would do it again, but she didn't, and soon she finished the article, folded it with care, and handed it back. "You are privileged," she said, "to be in the company of the most famous young woman in Paris. I am also very hungry. What have you in your box there?"

"Well," Michael replied, "I have sandwiches and olives and—" He dropped into a pit of silence, her last two sentences repeating themselves in his mind—clearly—precisely—and in English.

He twisted around, staring straight at her. Eyeball to eyeball. He felt very silly indeed, and because he felt silly, he also felt angry. And so he exploded. "Well I'll be a dirty shirt! Why didn't you *tell* me?"

She had the grace at least to look repentant, whether she really was or not. "Because I am a—how do you say? —a *fiend*. Everyone says so. 'What a fiend,' they say, 'that Danielle.' What *kind* of sandwiches?"

Stretching out a leg, Michael hooked his toe around the lunch box, drew it within reach of his hand, and set it on his right side where she couldn't reach it. "We'll talk about sandwiches," he said with rocklike firmness, "*after* you tell me what it's all about—why you ran away and all that. And I mean *you*—not old Clementine Whoosis!"

"Whoosis?" She repeated the word experimentally and laughed. "I like Whoosis. Another time I shall be Clementine Whoosis. But now I am Danielle de la Tour, just as the *journal*—the newspaper—says. You must call me Dani because all my friends do—and you are my friend because you have come to help me and to"— she managed to look sly—"to bring me sandwiches."

He tried to look severe and uncompromising but couldn't stop himself from grinning at her. Anyway, he realized he was very hungry, lunchtime or not. "Oh, all right," he said, setting the lunch box on his lap and flipping the catch. "How about peanut butter and jelly?"

She accepted a sandwich with an oddly formal *Je vous remercie*, and then switched back to English. "You have been very patient with me. I shall not play any more games now. You must ask me what you wish, and I will tell you." She took a dainty bite of her sandwich.

Michael took a not so dainty bite, at least in part to give himself a minute to think. This girl—this unpredictable, now-you-see-me-now-you-don't sort of girl—seemed to have given him a very odd feeling, old and new, familiar and unfamiliar all at the same time. All he could think of to compare it with was the sudden finding of something you had lost long ago and grieved over and given up for good. And it was like something else too—hey, this was crazy—it was like his discovery of Charly! Before he knew what he was going to say, he was saying, "You know what I called you all along? The prettiest gargoyle."

He didn't know what he expected her to say in reply. Something outrageous, probably. But after a moment she repeated the words consideringly: "Prettiest gargoyle." In the same tone she translated it: "*La plus belle gargouille.* I think I like that. It is a comfort to be the prettiest *something*." She took another bite and chewed contemplatively, looking intentionally smug.

Michael scowled to keep himself from grinning and cleared his throat resoundingly—a meeting-will-please-come-to-order sort of sound. "Anyway—now that we've got *that* all settled, here come the questions. First—"

"Tell me, Michael—what is your *other* name?"

"Horner," he said distractedly. "And now, if you'll please pay at—"

"Orn-air," she said. "Michael Orn-air. That is a very *in*-teresting name."

"It's an excruciatingly *gorgeous* name! *Now* will you tell me why you're hiding out up here and why you ran away from home?"

She gave him a sideways glance. "If I tell you," she said, "you will be angry with me."

"Angry! Why should I be angry? It didn't have anything to do with *me!*"

"Nevertheless," she said with calm certainty, "you will be angry."

He shook his head in exasperation. "Well, if you *don't* tell me I'll be forty times as angry."

She paused, considering. "If I do tell you, and you *are* angry with me, will you continue to be my friend?"

Michael nodded emphatically.

"And help me to hide from the police?"

"Well, sure."

"And from my uncle?"

"Naturally."

"And—and bring me peanut butter and jelly sandwiches?"

"Dozens! Now will you for gosh sakes *tell* me?"

"Very well." She brushed crumbs from her sweater and slacks with quick flipping movements of both hands, which she then folded primly in her lap. "I ran away from the home of my uncle," said Dani de la Tour, "because I refuse—I will not be *forced*—to go to America."

11

The Unseen Uncle

The silence between the two of them was so profound and went on so long that Michael became aware for the first time of how truly noisy a place he was in. The muted roar of a vast city bustling about its business was a never-ending sound. It filled the air so constantly that sometimes the ear mistook it for stillness and it could not be heard at all.

Then too, there were human voices. They were all around, faint but insistent. Some came from the other side of the tower. Tourist visiting was in full swing and had been for quite a long time. But the great bulk of the tower so deadened and distorted the sounds that they could have come from anywhere—from the street below, from within the bell chamber, or from the heavens above. There were even voices that seemed to come out of the very stones. (Later, when he really thought about it, he realized that those voices did come from inside the buttress at the corner of the tower merely feet away from where he was sitting. Inside this buttress was the stairway he himself had climbed to the tower's summit the day before.)

And so they sat, the two of them, amid this soundless din, mere feet away from scores of other people but as invisible as if they had been on another planet, and both of them considered for a time the things that went on in the most private fastnesses of all—their own two minds.

The first to find a voice, as might have been expected, was the prettiest gargoyle. She spoke softly, gloomily, apparently addressing the parapet in front of her. "I *told* him he would be angry, but he would not believe me. 'Why should I be angry?' he said."

"Well, I'm *not* angry," said Michael angrily. "I just don't get it, that's all."

"Get it?"

"Understand it. I don't *understand* it. What's so horrible about going to America?"

"'Orrible? Nothing is 'orrible. But—" She shrugged expressively. "But it is not France. It is not Paris."

"Well, of course it isn't. But it's not *Siberia*, for gosh sake! It wouldn't *kill* you to go there."

"Perhaps not. But I would not be happy there. All those Indians and bad men shooting the cowboys."

She shivered with revulsion, and Michael hooted. "That's only on television! I've never seen anybody shoot any cowboys, and I've lived in cattle country all my life!"

"Cattle country," she repeated, seeming to taste the words. "Where is this cattle country in which you live?"

"Oregon. Central Oregon. It's high country—just east of the Cascade Mountains." His words began to trip over each other in their eagerness. "I live in a town called Bend—actually at the edge of the town, and I've got a horse—well, he's not exactly *mine*, but I take care of him, and ride him, and. . . ." His voice trailed away as dawning suspicion quickly changed to certainty. "Indians and cowboys!" he exclaimed, not without admiration. "You're quite a subject changer, aren't you?"

Ignoring this irrelevant observation, she said, "You love this cattle country 'of yours—this Bend, this Oregon—very much. Not so?"

"Sure, but that's not—"

"You would not, of your own choice, leave it and come to live in Paris?"

"Okay, okay, I get the idea! But I came, didn't I? I didn't run away and hide up on a—"

"On a cathedral? No. But perhaps you would have run away and hidden on one of your mountains if it had not been your family—your mother and father—who said to you: 'You must go to Paris and live.' But if you had no family, and someone *else* had said you must go to Paris, then perhaps you would have run away."

Michael stared into her eyes, a little awed by their intensity. At some point during this last impassioned speech she had performed with apparent ease a complicated maneuver that lifted her from her seat beside him to a kneeling position directly in front of him. "But you," he protested, "you have *some* family. You have your uncle."

"No-no-no-no!" She shook her head with startling violence. "I have *not* my uncle—my uncle has *me!* He does not want me, but he has me. He is—how do you say—you have an expression"— she raised both hands, fingers outspread, and waggled them in swift, frustrated little arcs on either side of her face as she struggled to think of the words she wanted—"he is stricken with me—no, that is not right."

"Stuck? He's *stuck* with you?" Michael supplied the word reluctantly, but she nodded vigorously. "Yes—that is it! Since my father and my mother were killed, he has been stuck with me."

She wasn't asking for sympathy but merely stating a fact, but Michael felt that a crumb of comfort might not be amiss. "Well," he said, "I guess as far as that goes, my parents are stuck with *me*."

She brushed that aside. "You know it is not the same."

Michael did know, so he tried something else. "Here. How about some sody-pop?"

She did a semi-cartwheel back to the sleeping bag and accepted the proffered bottle. "Sody-pop?" she said.

He explained about sody-pop, then shifted the subject back to where it had been. "Your uncle—how come he wants you to go to America?"

She shrugged, indicating that the subject didn't deserve much attention. "Because he is going to open another factory there."

"Is he—is he mean to you?"

"Mean?"

"Unkind. Does he mistreat you?"

She laughed, but is wasn't a happy laugh. "No, no—he is *never* unkind. He is always kind. Kind-kind-kind-kind! He is very rich and he gives me everything I want. That way he does not have to—to—" She frowned horrendously and fluttered her hands again as she burrowed for the English words to express her thoughts. Finding them, her face cleared, and she produced them triumphantly. "That way he does not have to *get mixed up with me!*"

"My gosh!" Michael exclaimed, somewhat in awe of this uncle, who must be made of plastic or something. "You strike me as a person who'd be pretty hard *not* to get mixed up with."

She laughed, and this time it was a gay sound. "That was a lovely thing to say, Michael!"

Now it was his turn to frown. "Call me Mike, will you? And I wasn't trying to say anything *lovely*." Quite suddenly he arrived at the conclusion that it was time to get down to a few practical matters. "Okay," he said, "leaving out of it the reasons *why* you ran away, and why you don't want to go to America, what we've got to think about is what happens next. Even if you don't get caught you can't hide up there forever. Have you thought of that?"

"But of course! I am not *imbécile!*"

"Didn't say you were. So what's your plan?"

"Very simple. But very clever. I shall send a letter to my uncle."

"Send a letter! Well, for gosh sake, how—" Seeing her cock her head toward him, eyes slyly aslant, Michael scented a trap before he had quite stepped into it, and choked off his comment.

"It will be like this." She finished her sandwich, brushed away crumbs either real or imaginary, and locked her arms around her knees. "I wrote the letter before I left home. It is—" She gestured toward the eastern corner of the tower. "—it is around the corner, with the rest of my things. It says this: 'My dear Uncle Fernand, I am safe and well, but I am beyond your reach. I will return on one condition— that you promise you will not force me to go to America.

If you will promise, instruct Mam'selle—' Mam'selle is my governess. '—instruct Mam'selle to go on our usual walk each night, at half past eight, wearing her hat with the flowers. I have friends who will be watching. If she comes they will inform me and I will return.'"

Dani favored her patient listener with a brilliant smile. "That is all. It is signed: *'Ton fermement resolu Danielle.'* Which means I am absolutely determined—yes?"

"Yes," Michael said. "*Now* tell me how you were going to mail it?"

"Were?"

"Yes—*were*. I'll mail it, now that I'm around. But what if I hadn't showed up?"

"Very simple. Very clever." Her face was laughing at him—without sound. "Every day hundreds of foreigners come here. Many are the age of you and me, or nearly so. I simply find a pleasant boy or girl—Italian, German, Dutch, English—and I say—"

"Don't tell me," Michael interrupted, "you speak *all* those languages?"

She shrugged. "There is always *one* language two can speak. So I say to this girl, this boy, 'I wish to play a joke on my uncle. Will you please to help me?' They will agree and I will find out how soon they are returning to their own country. If it is within a day or two I say, 'Please post this letter from your home without telling anyone about it.' I impress upon them that to post this letter is of greatest importance.

"So they go on their way, and very soon my uncle receives a letter from Milan—Dusseldorf—Amsterdam—London—and there is great mystery, great excitement. Dani is in Milan! How can she ever be found? We must do as she says! Mam'selle—put on your hat with the flowers this evening and walk!

"So Mam'selle walks from the apartment of my uncle to the promenade down there between Notre Dame and the Seine—while up here Danielle de la Tour and the *rest* of the gargoyles are watching. . . "

At this point, reaching the limit of her tolerance for inaction, she sprang up with the effortless motion Michael now recognized as characteristic of her and flung herself over to the parapet where she glared fiercely down at the scene below—"are watching with our wicked eyes!"

Michael was scrambling to his feet when she whirled back, flinging out her arms. "And *voilà!* I see Mam'selle in her hat—and the message is delivered! All is well. I do not have to go to America. And in the morning I descend from the tower. I go home to find my uncle waiting. He—"

She paused, and Michael felt a subtle change in her, as if she were capable of making a person aware of some certain feeling just by feeling it.

She went on. "He is not the same, my uncle. He has changed. He has changed forever. He has discovered in this time of—of fear and trouble that this Danielle—this child of his brother, this so funny little bird that he must shelter in his house—was living and warm and full of wishes.

"He has learned, my uncle, that when this bird flies away, a loss and sadness come to live with him. He sits alone and he thinks, 'Perhaps I should have regarded her with more attention, with more care. Perhaps I have made a terrible mistake! Perhaps I am not very wise.' "

With difficulty Michael tore his eyes away from the small face that hovered above him. The sun was high now, almost directly overhead, and it made seeing difficult, but there was no mistaking the tears that glistened in her eyes. Actress though this girl undoubtedly was, these were no cried-to-order tears. They came—as Dad had once said long ago of tears of Michael's own—"from the bottom of the well." Funny he should remember that now. Funny, too, that he should be possessed of an insistent hankering to punch this Uncle Fernand smack in the middle of the stomach.

12

The Friendly
Garbage Man

Uncle Fernand, being absent, was unpunchable, but the need remained for some kind of action. And it had better, Michael decided with a sound instinct he didn't know he possessed, be something very impersonal and prosaic.

Accordingly, in the most stolid, unimaginative, Charlyish manner he could contrive, he scooped into a heap all the objects he had left lying around him, including the jacket. From one pocket of that he extracted the iron nut, at the same time slipping his handkerchief from a hip pocket and holding it wordlessly aloft without looking up.

It was taken from his hand, and Michael made a huge project out of tying one end of the ball of twine to the nut. He even grunted a bit as he pulled the knot tight, to

show how hard he was working at it. Then a small brown
hand appeared in front of his nose, with the balled-up
handkerchief in it. "*Vois-tu*, Mike," she said. "You see—
the prettiest gargoyle is also the most stupid. What are you
doing?"

"Tying this"—grunt—"string onto this"—grunt—"nut."

"Oh," said Dani. She sank to her knees in front of him
and sat back on her heels. "And what will you do with it
then?"

"I won't do anything with it," he replied. "*You* will."
Things were comfortably back under control now. There
were practical matters to deal with, and he was in charge.
"After it gets dark tonight, you'll go to the railing—right
over there—and let the string down till you feel it touch
bottom. That'll put it where it'll be awful hard to see—
clear back in the recess between the two buttresses.
Then—"

"Hah! I know!" He looked up to see that her eyes
were shining, but no longer with tears. "I will let the string
down. You will be waiting below. You will fasten peanut
butter and jelly sandwiches to the string!"

He grinned. "Well, food anyway. And things to drink.
Whatever you need. And I'll send messages too—in case
there's something you ought to know about. But I've got
to be real cagey because—"

"Cagey? What is cagey?"

"Clever. Clever in a sneaky way. In the first place,
there's my folks—my family. It wouldn't do for them to
find out what I'm up to. And then there's the police!
You'd better believe they're really looking for you. I'll bet
by this time every cop in Paris has got a copy of that
picture in his pocket."

She drew herself up, managing to look regal even while

still on her knees and wearing stretch pants and a sweater.
"Young man," she announced, "you are very fortunate to
be associated with a person of so great the importance."

"Well, I won't be associated with you very long if you
go on cavorting around up here in front of a lot of tourists,
and wearing that neon sweater, and sneezing at the wrong
time— Hey, I forgot to ask! How come you were up there
in the bell—"

He got no further because she had loosed another peal
of laughter like the one he had wished would be repeated,
and when it ended, she said, "I shall remember always the
sounds you made—those sneezes! I stuffed my mouth
with this so-bright sweater, and I nearly exploded my head
to smother my laughing!"

Michael permitted himself a modest chortle at the
thought of how clever he had been, then started to repeat
his question. But she was ahead of him. "When I first came
to the tower, the weather was very bad. It rained. The
wind blew. Up there inside the tower it was sheltered and
dry. But I do not like it up there—inside—in the night."
She shivered, and her face turned somber. "Things creak
and thump, and the wind cries of sad and fearsome
things." The shadow passed over her face and was gone.
"But now the weather is fine, and I prefer to be in the
open where I can see the sky, and the stars, and below, the
lights of Paris—"

"Yeah!" Michael exclaimed, putting a stop to this
poetic flight with deliberate inelegance. "Out in the open
where anybody with a telescope can see you! No fooling,
you've got to start being a little more careful—and it might
as well be now. Here—put this on!" He stood up and held
out his jacket.

Somewhat to his surprise she raised no objection but

slipped into it and, wrapping it tight around her, struck an extravagant pose, like a fashion model. "Very chic, is it not?" she brightly inquired.

"Absolutely stunning," Michael agreed. He picked up Old Longview and stepped over to the parapet, adding, "Now I'll explain a few things."

As she joined him, he rested the spyglass on the railing and aimed it toward the balcony across the river from which not so very long ago he had been aiming it in exactly the opposite direction. After a moment the balcony's iron railing swung into the magic circle. Then, holding the glass in place, he stepped aside. "Now you look," he said.

Dani exclaimed with astonishment. "But it is so near! It is at the end of my arm!"

"That's where I live," Michael said and went on in a businesslike manner. "Now look at the sheet of paper at the side. You see the letter *M?*"

"Yes. One, two, three, four of them."

"Not five?"

"N—no. Only four."

"But you can read the fourth one all right?"

"Easily."

"Okay, I'll write with letters that size."

"Letters?"

He explained. It took a long time because Dani was always a small jump ahead of him—at times a jump in the wrong direction—but right or wrong she greeted each new aspect of his planning with enthusiasm that bordered on the violent, so that he spent much of the time calming her down and getting her pointed in the right direction.

Old Longview was to remain with her, a development which sent her into what Michael recognized as ecstasy.

She was to focus it on Michael's balcony at intervals during the daylight hours, and if he had anything to communicate, he would print it in discernible letters and tape it to the side of the building where his M sheet was now.

If she, on the other hand, wished to communicate with him, it involved more complicated procedures and must be done at night. The little flashlight figured prominently in this maneuver. If the need to communicate arose, Dani was to flash the light three times, and because it would be impossible for Michael to maintain a constant watch she was to make this signal on the hour and again on the half hour, so that if he were unable to be watching at one time, he probably could at the other.

After signaling, she would let down the weighted twine with a note fastened to it by means of his Scotch tape. Hidden in the recess between the two buttresses at the bottom of the building, the note would await the arrival of Michael, who would get there either slowly or swiftly, depending on the movements of parents and policemen. He would then read the note and take whatever action it called for.

Next, to facilitate daytime communication, Michael was to become the unofficial artist in residence on the towers of Notre Dame. Equipped with sketchbooks and drawing pencils, he would pursue his gargoyle studies on the spot instead of by telescope. Thus the *gardien* and anyone else who might be taking a more than touristy interest in the towers would become so accustomed to the sight of him that he could pop up almost anywhere—or on the other hand, disappear—without anyone's thinking twice about it. In addition to all that, he would have a lot more gargoyles to draw, so many of them being invisible from his balcony.

This was important. It was important for reasons of

strategy, of course, but that was far from the end of it. It was all very strange. Even though his life had suddenly become inextricably entangled with a dark-eyed gargoyle made of flesh and bone, he still found himself possessed by an unexplainable fascination with those made of stone. Maybe someday he would understand it all.

"Someday," however, would have to take care of itself. Right now there were practical things to do. All explanations had been given, all arrangements made, and he was now prepared to undertake his first mission on behalf of the prettiest gargoyle—a foray into the world of people, to replenish her depleted supply of food and drink.

The first step in this operation involved negotiating the two gargoyle-guarded balconies at the southeast corner of the tower, in order to arrive at the eastern exposure that looked down on the steep cruciform roof of the cathedral. Dani, with Old Longview grasped carefully in both hands, led the way, and upon arriving at the eastern parapet, she whirled to face him with a brilliant smile. "*Voici! Le nid d'oiseau!*"

"*Nid*," Michael repeated. "Meaning 'nest'?"

She nodded and he grinned. "Looks more like a mare's nest than a bird's."

"Mare's nest?"

"Never mind. No time to explain." He bent and picked up the largest in the helter-skelter assortment of objects that lay scattered in a semicircle in the middle of the walkway. This was a backpack of the sort used by hikers. The scattered objects included empty bottles labeled "Limonade" and "Éau Evan"; a pile of wadded-up wrapping paper; a string shopping bag; a small stack of paperback books, on top of which rested the harmonica; a folding stool; a number of cans of varying shapes and sizes, both empty and unopened; and a folded-up blanket lying beneath a more or less neatly stacked collection of garments.

Slinging the pack over his shoulders, he adjusted the straps and presented his back to his companion. "Fill it up," he said. "Your friendly garbage man."

"Garbage?"

"*Service de nettoiement*," Michael said, quoting the words painted on all Parisian garbage trucks.

She rewarded this feeble pleasantry with a laugh and began stuffing the pack with bottles and other refuse. While she performed this chore, he peered off to the east, seeing the city now from a new vantage point, and he had to admire once more the care with which Dani had chosen her outdoor retreat.

This side of the tower was open to view only from the sky or from the roof of the cathedral and the spire that soared up from its center. Behind the cathedral lay the open space of the Square of the Archbishop, then the diagonal strip of river dividing the Île de la Cité from the smaller Île St. Louis. The latter, of course, was crowded with apartment buildings, but their distance and the superior height of the cathedral made it unlikely that anyone, even with a telescope, could get a clear view of whoever might be standing behind the railing where Michael now stood. Here the illusion of isolation from all one's fellow creatures except the pigeons was complete. Yet all one needed to do was walk a few steps, turn a few right angles, squeeze behind a gargoyle, and—presto—people! In a few moments Michael was going to do exactly that. But first . . . .

Once the friendly garbage man's pack was loaded and buckled up, and once he had slapped his shirt pocket to make sure the shopping list was there, and once he had hemmed and hawed a little, he faced his small companion with slightly beetled brow and an air of uncompromising determination. "Now look," he said, "I've been thinking."

Dani nodded. "I know. I could hear you thinking. You are a very loud thinker."

He beetled his brow a little more. "What I was thinking is serious. Things can happen, you know. You could get sick—like appendicitis or something—and *have* to go home. Or I could get sent away and not be able to help you." He pointed across the river to the stream of traffic along the quays. "Or one of those crazy drivers could mash me flat before I ever get the stuff for you. Or the cops could grab me and make me tell where you are— Now wait—don't get all worked up!" He had seen the light of drama dawning in her eyes. "Nothing's going to happen. But something *could*—and if it did, the worst that could happen is your uncle would make you go to America, and maybe *that* wouldn't be as bad as you think. That's all I'm saying."

She started to shake her head, but he didn't give her a chance to speak. "You don't have to agree with me. Just *think* about it, that's all. After all, look at me—up until a few days ago I couldn't stand this place, and now—" He halted, teetering on the brink of a cliff he hadn't known was there.

"Yes—and now?" The gaze she turned on him was so sweetly innocent that he knew it wasn't innocent at all.

"Nothing!" he said, but his voice sounded so grumpy that he added hastily, "Just remember things can change. *We* change!" The last words were no sooner spoken than he realized they weren't his words at all; they were his father's. This demoralized him so completely that he was vastly relieved when Dani suddenly gasped, clutched her stomach with both hands, and staggered backward. "Oh!

You must hurry—I am ill—I suffer—I have the appendicitis! "

"Okay, I'm going," Michael said. "I'll bring a doctor." He hunched his shoulders to settle the pack on his back and made his grin fiendish. "On second thought, I'll just bring a *knife!*"

Her laughter trailed him as he followed the walkway along the series of right-angle turns that would take him to the north side of the tower where the tourists were sure to be.

Following Dani's advice, he dropped to hands and knees as he reached the second and last balcony. Here he was effectively, if not completely, concealed by the ornamental masonry which supported the parapet's railing. He crawled along the parapet until he reached the inner corner with its iron barrier, and there he crouched, peering through the apertures in the fretwork. Just a few feet away was the bell gallery door through which he had made his noisy exit—could it have been only yesterday? The door was closed now, and for the moment the only people to be seen were moving along the walkway between the two towers. They all were jabbering away, staring, pointing toward the panorama to the west. The trouble was that at any moment one or more of them might turn and glance in Michael's direction. Not only that, others could abruptly turn the corner from the walkway along the front of the north tower. Worst of all, the *gardien* himself might appear just as abruptly.

But Michael couldn't wait for a sure thing. Right now nobody, as far as he could tell, was looking in his direction. Gathering his legs under him, he lunged upward, grabbed the jutting elbows of the gargoyle in charge of that particular corner, and hoisted himself to the level of the railing where he compressed himself into the impossibly narrow gap between the gargoyle's elbows and the wickedly pointed top horizontal bar of the barrier. A second later he dropped to his feet on the other side of the grille, straightened—and found himself staring into a pair of bright black Oriental eyes.

The eyes belonged to a boy of perhaps eight or nine who had appeared from behind a gargoyle at the far corner of the railing beside which Michael now stood. Now he stared with an unblinking gaze in which there was no expression whatsoever. Suddenly realizing that he himself was staring in the same manner, Michael manufactured a fairly convincing grin, topped it off with a conspiratorial wink, and put a finger to his lips.

This elaborate pantomime worked. The youngster grinned and winked in turn; then with loud shushing noises and finger to lips he turned and disappeared around the corner of the tower. Michael heaved a sigh of relief. Perhaps, he thought, some of Dani's theatrical ability was rubbing off on him. He strolled along the parapet, gawking like any other tourist just to be on the safe side, and plunged at last into the stairwell up which he had climbed that morning. First stop—a trash receptacle. *Service de nettoiement.*

13

Wealth for the Asking

The rest of the afternoon passed as swiftly as the morning had, and as the dinner hour approached, Michael made his way home, feeling as if he had done a real day's work.

Actually, now that he thought about it, it hadn't been exactly easy. Two trips up to the towers and down again involved a lot of legwork, not to mention the fancy gymnastics required to climb around iron barriers at top speed but avoid detection by the casually curious.

In between the first descent and the second ascent had come a lot of scurrying around from shop to shop over on the Right Bank to find the various items on Dani's shopping list. This would not have been particularly difficult—most of the items were food and bottled drinks—if the list had not included batteries for her little radio. The radio was of Swiss manufacture, and the batteries, an odd size, were hard to come by. He had to go to half a dozen shops before he found them.

In addition to all the stair climbing and pavement pounding, there was the mental strain—equally tiring—of enduring what he imagined to be the cold-eyed scrutiny of every policeman he saw. It seemed as if he never escaped the sight of one before another came in sight. Though he kept telling himself what he really knew to be true—that there was almost nothing less visible to a policeman than a strolling boy—he couldn't banish the thought that sooner or later a steely grip would close on his arm and a stern voice would say, "A-*ha!* You are carrying the backpack of Danielle de la Tour—come with me!"

Even now, after he had returned the pack to its owner and descended the interminable stairs for the second time, he couldn't get over the idea that somewhere about his person was a clue to the whereabouts of number one on the most-wanted list of the French police. If he failed to exercise the utmost care the law would pounce and the jig would be up.

Pounce or no pounce, though, jig or no jig, there had been a moment when he would gladly have turned her over to the first cop he saw. He grinned now, thinking about it. He had just finished carving a niche for himself by becom-ing history's first (it seemed safe to assume) boy ever to deliver groceries to the towers of Notre Dame and had sat down on Dani's sleeping bag to rest his weary legs. And since it was on his mind, he brought up again the subject of America.

"You know," he had said, trying to sound as though it

had just that minute occurred to him, "I think I'm beginning to like Paris pretty well."

Busy making a neat pile of the things he had brought,
she looked up, faintly surprised. "But of course!" she
said.

"Well, don't be so smug. As I told you, about three days
ago I hated it."

"Aha! But *then* you had not met"— sticking her
thumbs in her mouth, forefingers at the corners of her
eyes, she stretched her face out of shape—"the prettiest
gargoyle!"

He frowned severely. "Quit clowning, will you? What
I'm trying to say is—"

Suddenly she was on her feet in front of him, fists
jammed into the pockets of his old jacket, dark eyes huge
with seriousness. "I *know* what you are trying to say!
You are trying to say that if I go to America, my mind will
be changed, as yours has been. I will find a friend, as you
have done. I will become fond of San Francisco, and
everything will be—"

"*San Francisco!*" Michael was nearly shouting. "Why
didn't you *say* that's where you're going?"

"Because it is *not* where I am going. I told you I—"

"All right, all right! But it makes a difference!"

"It does not make a difference to *me.*"

Michael scrambled to his feet. Being seated gave the
other person all the advantage in an argument. "Well, it
would if you weren't too stubborn to even listen to what
I'm saying!"

They traded glare for glare. "I am not stubborn," Dani
declared after a pause. "I am"— she searched visibly for
the right word—"I am . . . *resolute!*" She produced this

rather high-flown word with an air so triumphant it was comical and Michael had to laugh. At that she smiled uncertainly. "Is that not the proper word—resolute?"

"Boy, is it the proper word! You're probably the most *resolute* person I ever knew. You're so *resolute* you make a donkey look wishy-washy! You—"

"Wishy-washy?"

He grinned. "Just what it sounds like." He glanced at his watch and added, "Wow! I've got to get the heck down from here. I *resolutely* don't want to get locked up for the night."

This time he had managed the complicated process of departure without any unexpected encounters, and now, still wryly marveling at the *resoluteness* of Danielle de la Tour, he crossed to the Left Bank whence he had come that morning and found a newsstand where he bought two papers—*France-Soir* for his father, and for himself the Paris *Herald*, which was published in English for Americans. Then he crossed the street to the little park and plunked himself down on a bench to rest his legs and read what the *Herald* had to say about the most wanted girl in Paris.

First, though, he glanced automatically toward the cathedral, which was awash now in the gentle light of approaching evening. He let his eye wander along the lines and curves and angles of the towers, and had been staring in this absentminded way for some time before he woke to the startling realization that his eye had made a discovery quite independently of his mind. And it was a sort of important discovery. Not the discovery itself, exactly, but rather the fact that he had made it—and with no prompting from anybody. It was simply this:

All those fantastic gargoyles had been put up there for a very definite purpose. They weren't up there just to be amusing, or fascinating, or frightening, though they were all those things; they were there because the building *couldn't do without them.* Not that it would fall down, of course, but it just wouldn't *look* right. It was the same with the true gargoyles—those openmouthed waterspouts jutting out from the corners of the tower high above, where the great bell hung. Those creatures and the chimeras below, like Charly, were there to play tricks on the eye, to slow it down or make it stop when it tended to follow a vertical line straight up or a horizontal one straight out until it got away from the cathedral altogether.

This was something you couldn't see when you were close by, but at this distance the monsters were indistinguishable from one another and were simply shapes made of stone like the rest of the structure, and they had had a function, a job to do. By squinting a little and using his imagination, Michael made the gargoyles vanish, and the towers were no longer the same. They were still square and solid and grand, but their outlines were bare and harsh and unwelcoming to the eye. When he stopped squinting, the whole building restored itself, and the eye could look and be satisfied once more.

With a kind of shivery awe Michael thought of the man, all those hundreds of years ago, in whose mind this vast structure had existed before ever the first stone was laid down. Had he known even then that gargoyles would be needed on those towers? And if so, *how* had he known? How could any man know so much? And how had he known—this architect of long ago—that huge masses of stone propping up the walls could be made to look air-borne and weightless and swooping? To be such a man, to know such things, to see such a thing in your mind as a cathedral, and to build it, would be like—and here Michael really did shiver a little—would be like, in a small way, being God.

No telling how long he might have sat lost in this shivery but not very useful reverie if his ear hadn't caught the sound—faint, then swelling, then faint again—of one of those hee-hawing vehicles of the police, bringing him quickly back to the world of now. Guiltily he began looking through the pages of the *Herald*.

Events of a turbulent world, as it turned out, had crowded the Case of the Missing Niece off the front page, but on page three this headline leaped out at him:

GIRL'S DISAPPEARANCE
PROMPTS REWARD OFFER

As his eyes raced over the print below, Michael said softly, "Wow!"

The wow was a humble salute to the fact that Uncle Fernand, described in the news story as a "textile tycoon," had offered a reward of fifty thousand francs for information leading to discovery of the whereabouts of his niece. Such information, the story went on to say, would be held in strictest confidence. It further outlined the simple steps to follow in delivering such information.

Michael read the rest of the story automatically. It didn't say much anyway, beyond the fact that the police had "clamped a tight lid" on all information, comment, or speculation on whether or not kidnapping or other foul play was involved.

Being the one person besides Danielle de la Tour herself who wasn't concerned with kidnappers, Michael could ignore the rest of the story and return to that lovely round figure—fifty thousand francs. This made him, it now occurred to him, probably the only person in Paris, or France, or Europe, or the whole world, who could have those nine thousand dollars just for the asking. All he had to do was hold out his hand, so to speak, and old Big Shot Fernand de la Tour would plunk nine thousand bucks into it. No questions asked. Instant riches.

The Horner family's Parisian interlude was being financed—and on a shoestring at that—by a grant from a scholarly foundation, plus the borrowing of every last nickel Dad and Mom could lay their hands on. Like most boys brought up in households where there is never quite enough money for everything, Michael had dreamed his share of dreams in which he stumbled upon great treasure. Usually these dreams began in a modest way. He would find a nickel or a dime, then more nickels and dimes scattered all over the ground. Then quarters and half dollars. (Oddly, there was never any paper money.) The quarters and halves would proliferate while Michael madly scrambled to pick them up and stuff them into pockets. It was always the horrible realization at last that he could never scramble fast enough to pick them *all* up that brought him wide awake and just as poor as ever. It was always a marvelous experience while it lasted, but the awakening was awful.

And now here he was—wide awake—no dream—and nine thousand dollars was his for the asking. Eighteen thousand half dollars, thirty-six thousand quarters, ninety thousand dimes. . . .

Imaginations being as impossible to control as dreams, there was nothing Michael could do about what his own was up to now. It raced like wildfire through all the usual daydream material—ice-cream sundaes by the bucket, acres

of chocolate bars, whole supermarkets full of skiing equip-
ment, silver-studded saddles and bridles, outboard motors,
a swimming pool in the backyard—and finally steadied
down to the really important things.

There was the combination gas-and-electric kitchen
Mom was ready to part with her eyeteeth for. Or an
addition to the house so there could be a study for Dad
and a guest room. Or the education fund. In the Horner
household the education fund ranked number one of the
list of Things to Be Worried About. It was the fund that
was supposed eventually to send both Lucinda and Michael
to college. Every payday since Lucinda was born, Dad had
put a few dollars, or just a few cents, into it. The money
was drawing interest and was growing, but so slowly that
Mom and Dad often got discouraged. Dad joked about it,
telling Michael that by the time he was ninety there should
be enough to get him through his freshman year, but he
was worried all the same, because of the way the price of
education kept going up.

The busy old imagination now presented a dramatic
little scene starring Michael Horner, with Professor Frede-
rick Horner in a supporting role. The dialogue—a monologue, actually—had only one line, and it went like this:

"Oh, by the way, Dad, here's a little something for the
old education fund." Accompanying action consisted of
Michael's casually tossing onto the desk in front of his
careworn father a check for fifty thousand francs.

He even made a stab at a second line, which would start
off: "In five years, at five percent compounded annually,
this will amount to—" Fortunately he didn't know how to
figure compound interest. If he had known, this little
playlet might have turned into a whole evening's entertain-
ment.

As it was, he simply woke up from the daydream—with just a shade of regret—to the certain realization that not for fifty thousand francs, or fifty million, would he blow the whistle on Dani de la Tour.

He folded his papers together, got up from the bench, and headed for home across the little park. Funny, he thought, what a difference a few hours could make in a person's whole life. Only a few hours ago—when Dani was nothing to him but the prettiest gargoyle, a face in the magic circle of an antiquated telescope—he could have dashed off to the big textile tycoon without a second thought and told him where his wayward niece was to be found. The money would have come pouring into his hands, and things would have been forever different in the house of Horner.

Now, of course, he couldn't do it because Dani was his friend—a very special sort of friend—and a person simply didn't sell his friends down the river for money. Her adventure was his adventure now, and however it might all turn out, Michael Horner was going to see it through to the end. He no longer had any choice.

And so—because having no choice is often a lot more comfortable than having one—he was very comfortable indeed as he let himself out the gate of the little park, crossed Poor Julian Street, and climbed the stairs to the apartment, where to his amazement he found his family awaiting him impatiently and en masse.

The first to speak, naturally, was Lucinda, whose contribution was, "Well, for heaven's sake where have you *been?*"

Next, Mom, who looked as if she wanted to laugh but felt like crying: "Whatever have you done, Mike, to deserve such wonderful parents!"

And last, but a couple million light-years from least, Dad, who wore a lopsided sort of grin:

"Well, boy, you might as well start packing your bag. You're going home!"

14

The Lighted Fuse

About a year before, Michael had been kicked square in the stomach by a frisky filly he was trying to catch. The sensation, a memorable one in all respects, seemed to be repeating itself now. The only difference was that now he was standing on his feet instead of lying flat on his back in an Oregon pasture. Otherwise everything was much the same: All the air had abruptly left his lungs, and there was no chance of getting any more again, ever; a kind of wind was taking a shortcut straight through his head instead of going around it in the usual manner; and his eyes were not seeing anything much.

This state of suspended animation lasted an incredible length of time while Michael struggled reluctantly to come to grips with the idea that something was expected of him, that all those eyes in all those faces were watching him, waiting for him to say something. A word or something like that. After a while he thought of a word and how to say it. "Home?" he said.

Mom laughed. It was an excited laugh, but amused too. "Yes, Mike—home! H-o-m-e—on the range—where the heart is—be it ever so humble."

Lucinda laughed, too. "Really, Michael, you should see your *face*. You look like you had a mouthful of worms!"

"A very accurate comparison, Cindy," Dad said. "Come sit down, Mike, and I'll tell you what it's all about."

Mom turned brisk. "You've got about ten minutes before dinner's ready. Come lend a hand, Cindy."

Michael, like a person under hypnosis, took the chair his father indicated, and listened. "I still can't believe it," Dad began.

What he couldn't believe, his story disclosed, was that at lunch only the day before he had been introduced by a mutual friend to a young Swiss geologist whose specialty was the study of volcanoes. That part of it wasn't hard to believe. In the scholarly world Dad inhabited a Swiss volcanologist was no surprise. At the Sorbonne he had met a Turkish mathematician, a Hindu biochemist, a Bolivian physicist, a Taiwanese philologist, and no telling how many other exotic specimens. The unbelievable part was that the young Swiss, discovering where Professor Horner came from, had all but swallowed his saucer in the excitement. The one small spot on the face of the earth where above all others he would rather be for two or three months was Bend, Oregon, U.S.A. Bend, he said, was the center of an area in which were situated some of the world's most recently formed lava fields and other volcanic phenomena.

The Swiss and his wife could manage the air fare to Portland, with very little left for them to live on. But he would do, he said, *anysink*—he would dig ditches, he would. . . .

But he would not have to dig ditches because here, like a genie loosed from his bottle, was the American professor who had a house in Bend, Oregon, with enough land so that a frugal Swiss scholar could grow vegetables and with fruit trees of various kinds besides. And so, instead of digging ditches, the volcanologist, to whom this American professor had taken an enthusiastic liking, would have to do nothing in return for all these heaven-sent amenities but provide a congenial home, three meals a day, and a minimum of supervision of a thirteen-year-old boy who was really quite self-sufficient.

The volcano expert, going into a state of prolonged eruption, had arranged for another luncheon meeting today, this time bringing his wife, whose virtues and accomplishments far exceeded his descriptive powers in the so-difficult English language. Even at her young age she was one of the finest cooks in all Lausanne, and she was absolutely *wunderbar* with boys, having helped raise *sree yoong brooders. Sree!*

The American professor had taken a liking to the wife, too, and so it was all arranged. It was now Friday. The volcano man could wind up his Paris affairs on Saturday, make plane reservations, and be ready, *feerst sing Zunday*, to set off across the top of the world, nonstop, to Portland, Oregon.

"So there you are, Mike," said Dad. "Just as I said, get your bag packed—you're as good as on your way!"

Throughout his recital Michael's eyes had remained fixed on his father's face as if it were the last mirage in the desert. Like Charly (whom he felt he must resemble at this point), he couldn't even blink. But behind that feeble-minded façade the action was comparable to what goes on inside a steam boiler with the safety valve plugged. Super-heated molecules of thought were racketing around inside his skull at the speed of light, bouncing off one another and achieving nothing.

For practical purposes, however, this same mind oper-ated with all the agility of an enormously fat man getting out of a small bathtub, and it was a matter of measurable seconds before it registered on Michael that he had been asked a direct question. After another measurable second it was repeated. "I *said*," said the professor, "how do you like *them* apples?" He always took pride in his command of common speech.

Summoning a great deal of resolution and effort, Michael uttered his second word of the evening. "Great!" he said.

Next, he was aware that his father was looking at him in a puzzled way. "I expected a whoop or two of joy," he remarked, "or even a hallelujah."

Making a supreme effort to pull himself together, Michael pumped what he hoped was enthusiasm into his voice. "Well, I do think it's great! But it's just, well, you sprung it on me so fast I'm . . . just sort of bowled over!"

These bogus burblings were a miserable performance, Michael told himself, thinking what an artistic creation Dani de la Tour would have made of it. Inspiration nudged him. "I guess—I just can't *believe* it."

It worked. Dad nodded enthusiastic agreement. "Just what I was saying! It's basically an unbelievable set of circumstances, but there it is!"

"Yup, there it is!" agreed Michael idiotically, nodding his head too. Fortunately Mom chose that moment to call them to the table, where he managed to keep his mouth so full that coherent speech was virtually impossible. This produced a heated demand by Lucinda that he either stop eating like an absolute *pig* or leave the table. Skillfully escalating this confrontation, he brought down upon his own head and Lucinda's a parental command to maintain absolute silence for the rest of the meal.

This gave him a chance to think, which he needed more than anything else, but his thoughts were completely unproductive, and it was a relief when dinner was over at last.

Lucinda went to her room while Mom and Dad had their coffee, as usual, in the living room. Michael, doing his best to be nonexistent, sidled to the window that opened on the balcony and looked over toward Notre Dame. There was no signal light from the tower, of course, because there was still a little daylight left, and probably there would be no signal anyway. After all, Dani had everything she would need at the moment.

He wondered what she was doing right now. Eating? No, she had probably finished. Listening to the little radio with the new batteries? More likely she'd save that until later, when it was too dark to read. Right now she'd be reading one of her books or maybe playing a concert for herself on the harmonica. Or leaning on the parapet, looking toward his window, wondering what *he* was doing. . . .

In the room behind him a voice said, "Danielle de la Tour," and Michael felt himself turn rigid. An instant later he relaxed, wobbly with relief as he realized his father was merely reading the paper and telling Mom about it.

"The poor little thing!" said Mom. "I do hope she's just run away, instead of being kidnapped!"

"Not likely," Dad said. "They'd have found her by this time."

Michael sidled back into the room. Like the criminal returning to the scene of the crime, he didn't want to miss anything.

"Oh, what a ghastly thing!" Mom said, shaking her head. "If it were one of mine I'd—well, I'd just go to pieces." She sounded so distressed that Michael longed to tell her everything was all right, that Danielle de la Tour was in good hands. Namely, his. Or anyway she had been until the bomb was exploded just before dinner. He edged into a chair and listened.

In a moment Dad said, "The uncle has my sympathy. Think what he must be going through!"

This was too much for Michael. Forgetting he must reveal nothing, he spoke up. "How do you know he isn't just glad to get rid of her?"

Dad's startled eyes peered at him over the top of the newspaper and Mom said, "Mike! What a—a *peculiar* thing to say!"

"Well, it's possible," he said stubbornly but not very wisely. "After all, he's only her uncle. Maybe she's just a pain in the neck to him, and—"

Interrupting in his mildest tone, Dad said, "Then he must put a pretty high value on a pain in the neck. He's offering fifty thousand francs to anybody who can help find her."

"Fifty thousand francs!" Michael exclaimed scornfully. "I'll bet that's just chicken feed to him!" Having rejected this sum in his mind, he found it beginning to look pretty paltry. "I'll bet he could pay a hundred times that much and never know the difference. He just doesn't *want* to get her back!"

Dad put down his paper, and now both parents stared at Michael in considerable astonishment. Mom spoke first.

"Michael, I don't understand. Where did you get such a *perverse* idea?"

Belatedly he saw danger looming and scrambled frantically to avoid it, bitterly blaming himself for creating the necessity. "Well, I only read the paper, same as you, and—I dunno—this uncle just struck me as that kind of guy, that's all."

Dad greeted this flimsy explanation with a long silence. Once he started to say something but thought better of it. Then he turned the pages of the paper and after a moment said, "These earthquakes in Turkey—worse than the last ones."

Now Michael began calling himself names in earnest. *Why* had he gone flapping away with that big loose lip of his? It was a bad enough sign that Dad had so obviously changed the subject, but now he was doing something even more ominous. While, ostensibly, he went on reading the paper, his bristly brows squeezed closer together in a frown, and the long index finger of his right hand poked up and began slowly, rhythmically, tapping the point of his chin. These, Michael knew, were sure signs that his father was thinking very hard indeed, and on this particular occasion the subject of those thoughts was undoubtedly his son, Michael.

Mom too recognized the signs. She picked up the coffee cups and without a word took them to the kitchen, where she began cleaning up the dishes. Michael considered volunteering to help her, for the sake of getting out from under Dad's eye, but his normal caution had returned, and he refrained, knowing that such uncharacteristic willingness to help would only call further attention to himself. He located his current book and settled down with it, as inconspicuously as possible.

The book was a spy thriller. Blood by the bucketful and yards of high-level sneakery. But he was using it only to hide behind, and every time he stole a glance at Dad over the top of it he lost the place and kept reading the same paragraph over and over. It was no use either to try using this uncomfortable interval for some desperately needed thought about what in the world he was going to do.

Here he was, thanks to Dad's bombshell, as good as on his way home. Home, and everything the word meant— skiing and riding and ball games, and Chuck and Gordon and Big Sam and all the rest, and the pines and the mountains and the illimitable expanse of sky, and his own room with its old-shoe feeling and all the treasures in it that were treasures only to him, and the countless other things the word "home" meant. . . .

But to go meant walking out on Dani when he had just barely enlisted in her cause. It meant leaving her alone against the world. Well, what of it? She'd been alone before—hadn't she—and managed to set the whole city of Paris on its ear. On the other hand. . . .

But there was no use trying to think, or read, or anything else as long as Dad was sitting over there also pretending to read but actually following a train of thought that might lead no telling where. Michael sometimes felt as if his father had an almost supernatural power of arriving at the truth of a matter once he set his mind to it. But in this case it was an absolute impossibility to start with Michael Horner and arrive, by a process of thinking alone, at a small girl on top of a huge cathedral. All the same, he wished he could have even a hint of where Dad's mental processes were taking him. It might be possible then at least to distract him a little.

Dad chose that particular moment to lay aside the

paper, stretch his arms mightily before folding them behind his head and leaning back in a deceptively relaxed
position. "What have you been finding to do with yourself," he asked, "now that your time's all your own?"

Michael shrugged, trying to look relaxed too. "Nothing
much—just messing around."

Dad cocked an eyebrow, smiling a little. "Come on,
Mike. You can do better than that."

Michael thought of his drawings. He had been hoping to
hold them in reserve, for when things might get really
rough. "Well," he said reluctantly, "I've been doing some
drawings. Of the gargoyles over on the cathedral." He
added hurriedly, "I'm sure slow at it, though. Takes me a
long time to do one." Crafty, crafty Michael.

Dad nodded. "Using the little telescope, I understand."

"Yeah." Under cover of that laconic syllable, Michael
felt a stirring of panic. What was Dad leading up to? What
if he wanted to know where the spyglass was now? Plung-
ing into a diversionary move, he hurried to the desk across
the room and got out the sketchbook. "I'll show you."

Dad carefully examined the two drawings—the completed one of Charly and the half-finished one of the
hooded monster. After a while he looked up. "I'm impressed. *Really* impressed. Cindy told me you were doing
something exceptional, but I had no idea—" He let the
sentence die and looked back at the drawing of Charly.

Michael, like most people whose work is praised, made
deprecating noises, which his father interrupted with a further observation. "What's so impressive is the feeling
you've put into these. It's—well—it's beyond your years.
These creatures seem to have done something to you." He
gave his head a little shake, indicating inability to express
what he meant. "Fantastic, aren't they—the chimeras?"

Trust Dad, Michael thought, to know the proper word. He was casting about for a suitable reply when his father went on. "No one knows for sure why they were put up there on those towers, but one theory appeals to me: that they were believed, back in the Middle Ages, to breathe out into the upper air the accumulation of evil thoughts that men brought with them into the church. A bunch of spiritual safety valves, in a way."

"Maybe so," Michael put in with an eagerness he forgot to suppress, "but that's not the *real* reason why they're up there."

"No? Then what is?"

Haltingly at first but with growing confidence, Michael told about his discovery. Often in the past when he had tried to put into words some hard-to-express idea which he had embraced with great enthusiasm but little thought, it had fallen apart in the telling, coming to sound like a ridiculous and childish thing. But not this one. This time he knew he was right, but because there was something a little scary about being sure—absolutely *sure*—of what had gone on in the mind of a man who had been dead for eight hundred years, he ended with a note of wonder in his voice. "If he *hadn't* put those—those chimeras up there, and the gargoyles too, higher up, it would have *bothered* him. It—" here Michael actually squirmed a little, feeling an unconscious but quite genuine discomfort— "it would have made him feel like—oh, you know—a picture hanging crooked. So he had to put *something* up there. He didn't care if it was chimeras or something else so long as it was that *shape* and on those corners."

He fell silent, abashed at his volubility. Dad was staring at him with an expression impossible to read. He went on staring for such a long time that Michael would have been acutely uncomfortable if somewhere along the line he hadn't realized that the stare was no longer at him, but *through* him, at something that didn't exist in the here and now.

At last he said, "You know, Mike, the older I get, the more amazed I am at how much of what happens to every one of us depends on plain blind chance!"

Now it was Michael's turn to stare. What in the world had prompted that observation? His father proceeded to make it clear. "For example: If I hadn't been in a tearing hurry for no very good reason a good many years ago and stupidly sliced my hand down to the bone on a sardine can, I'd never have met your mother. I'll tell you the details some time if you want to know, but they don't really matter. Then another time—back in 1959, I think it was—if I'd mailed a certain letter as I should have done, instead of absentmindedly carrying it around in my pocket for three days, I'd never have gone to work in Oregon and you'd have been born in Massachusetts, and all our lives would be different as a result. And now."

He stopped and eyed Michael almost apologetically. "If I'm way out in left field you can tell me so. Anyway, if I hadn't run out of Lifesavers the other day, I wouldn't have been passing the shop where I saw the spyglass, so I wouldn't have got it for you, and if I hadn't got it for you, you wouldn't have discovered the chimeras, and if you hadn't done *that. . . .* "

He paused again, and Michael mentally finished the sentence. "I'd never have met Dani de la Tour."

That, of course, was not what his father had in mind. He leaned forward, looking very serious, each hand clasping a knee. "Michael," he said, and the use of the complete name was an indication of how serious he really was, "I have a strong feeling you may have discovered what you'll want to do with your life."

"I—" Michael had to swallow. "I *have?*"

Dad nodded. "I'd almost bet on it. Provided there's such a thing as a born architect."

Somehow Michael knew that this would be a time and a place he would remember always: Dad's long, spare frame leaning awkwardly forward in his chair, the sounds of the traffic on the streets below, the swans on the fireplace, looking faded again in the artificial light, the funny, ornate old clock on the mantel choosing that moment to strike whatever hour suited its wayward fancy, Mom out in the kitchen humming as she worked, the muffled slamming of a door somewhere else in the building. . . .

Architect—architect. The word bloomed splendidly in the air. Then Dad was speaking again. "I could have stared at those towers every day for the rest of my life and never have seen what you saw today—because it just isn't in me. . . . "

His voice, full of wonder, trailed away, and Michael's head turned toward the open window and the cathedral. It was swathed now in its soft golden nighttime garb. Hidden floodlights illumined its flat surfaces and turned its recesses into shadowed mysteries.

In the depths of one such mystery at the eastern corner of the south tower, his eye caught a speck of light that winked on and off, on and off, on and off.

Michael had a queer, breath-grabbing moment of panic. There was a fuse alight, sputtering along toward whatever lay at its end, and there was no way now to put it out.

15

Pursued!

Minutes later, as he descended the stairs with measured tread, Michael had already forgotten what excuse he had dreamed up for going out once more into the streets. Something about wanting to be alone to think, which sounded no less feeble for being at least partly true. The unstated reason, of course, was that he must respond to the signal from the tower.

The measured tread was a matter of appropriateness, of what was suitable. In his present mood, to go hurtling down the stairs with customary racket and abandon would have been as out of place as eating popcorn in church or whistling in the library. Anyway, he wanted to preserve this mood. It was a fine and solemn and significant thing—

and pretty scary as well. It surely couldn't happen more than once in a person's life—and for many not even once—to be told by no less an authority than one's father that one has just discovered, at the age of thirteen, one's life-work. And all because the father had run out of Lifesavers and ended up buying a telescope.

Dad's words repeated themselves: "And all our lives would be different as a result." Michael shivered a little, thinking of those Lifesavers and all that had changed—and was yet to change—because of them. Even if he didn't become an architect, he would always thereafter look at everything around him in a different way, resulting in countless other changes that couldn't even be guessed at now.

Nor would it end with him. There was Dani, too. Who could tell how much her whole life might be altered because of Michael Orn-air and his old brass telescope?

Reaching the street level, he let himself out the heavy leaded-glass door and closed it carefully behind him. As he crossed Poor Julian Street and began following the sidewalk along the edge of the little park, he shivered. There was a chill in the air now that the sun was down, and he wished he had brought a sweater. Even so, he found his steps slowing as he started across the Pont Double for the second time that day. Above and ahead the cathedral floated ponderously on its sea of shadow, luminous in the light of its hidden battery of moons.

In the middle of the bridge he came to a halt, glad to be diverted by the sight of a *bateau mouche* nosing its way through the center arch of the Petit Pont, next bridge to the west. He always liked to watch these huge glass-enclosed sight-seeing boats as they threaded their way through archway after archway in the endless series of

Seine bridges. Like vast, gay, colorful jukeboxes, they followed their leisurely course at intervals every day and far into the night, their amplifying systems alternating between musical selections and the voices of the tour guides as they explained the sights to their passengers in four different languages.

In these days of advancing spring, with the river imperceptibly rising, there was progressively less and less room beneath the bridges, and it was a thrill to watch how perilously close the plexiglass tops of the boats were coming to the unyielding stone of the bridges.

This time, though, he wasn't watching simply for the thrill, and he knew it. He was stalling, putting off for just a few moments longer the next contact with Dani. Why? Because even though the contact would be only by means of scribbled notes at the end of a string, he would have to tell her how everything had changed.

In one way, actually, a note on a string might be best. In a scribbled note you couldn't hem and haw and build yourself a breastworks of words to hide behind; you'd have to come right out flatfooted and say it. Like this: Day after tomorrow I'll be going home—to Oregon. I'll come tomorrow to say good-bye. After that you'll be on your own.

The thought of this straight-from-the-shoulder missive gave him no joy. The *bateau mouche*, ablaze with light, was heading straight toward him now along the narrow passage between the ancient island and the Left Bank, and he realized he didn't much care whether it scraped its top on the stones of the Pont Double or didn't. Tearing his eyes from the boat and his hands from the railing, he went reluctantly across the bridge.

At the open gate in the iron fence that extended along

the sidewalk southward from the corner of the cathedral, he paused a moment. Pretending to admire the statue of a bishop (or maybe a saint) set into a niche in the foremost of the three buttresses supporting the tower on its south side, he peered warily around. Though dark, it would still be hours before the people of Paris went to bed. Auto traffic moved in a steady rush along the Rue d'Arcole in front of the cathedral, drowning the voices of men and women strolling around the edges of the Parvis. Out in the center of that great open space, he caught sight of two or three policemen with the distinctive round hats and the short capes which made them a sort of trademark of Paris. None of them was looking his way, and he eased through the gate into the walkway that passed along the southern façade.

A moment later he was pressing himself into the shadowed recess between the huge central buttress housing the down stairway and the slightly smaller rearmost buttress. He groped along the rough stone surfaces for the twine he knew would be hanging there if Dani had followed his instructions. In the poor light the brown string would be invisible against the stone. Not until it occurred to him to look down at the stones on which he was standing did his eyes make out a small white object which turned out to be a much-folded sheet of paper fastened to the string with Scotch tape.

It was the work of a moment to remove the note, unfold it and smooth it out against the stone of the buttress, but then complications arose. Even when he eased his way out from the shadows, the light wasn't strong enough to read Dani's writing which, like most European writing, was to American eyes a little odd in a thin and slanty sort of way. He wished he had had sense enough to ask her to print her notes or else had brought a flashlight himself. Having done neither, he had no choice but to take the note out to the sidewalk and lean against the standard of a streetlamp to read it.

"I watched you," he read. "You look very sad, and I—"

Michael lifted his eyes and stared, puzzling, into the night sky. She *watched* him? *When* did she watch him?

Instantly he felt very foolish indeed. Old Longview, of course! Stupidly, it hadn't once occurred to him that he himself might show up inside the magic circle. If he could read the expressions on her face from across the river, so could she read his—straight through the open balcony door. It gave him a naked feeling. He read on.

"You look very sad, and I am filled with remorse. I say to myself: Michael, he is right. I am *not* resolute. I am instead *stubborn.* So I will make to you this promise: I will *think* about San Francisco. I do not say I will *go* there, you understand, but I will truly *think.*"

The note ended with *"à demain"* (till tomorrow), and was signed "D." Then there was a postscript. "I watched you from the back as you crossed the bridge. You have need of a haircut."

He was running a hand up the back of his neck before he realized what he was doing and jerked the hand away. First thing tomorrow he would repossess that telescope.

This frivolous thought was followed by a gloomy one. The time had now come when he must write a note of his own. He dug in his pocket and got out the stub of pencil he had brought along, but instead of getting on with the job, he stayed slouched against the light standard, staring unhappily at nothing while the traffic moved steadily along in front of him. Two things were trying to occupy his mind at the same time. One was the question whether or not he had really looked sad, and if so when? The other thing was the problem of how he could possibly write the words he had resolved to write, now that she had given in to him and promised at least to *think* about going to America.

The answer to that one was, he couldn't. No matter what the consequences, he couldn't coldly send a note up to that lonely tower saying he must go away and leave her to her fate. No, he'd have to do it in the morning—face to face and with whatever hemming and hawing it would take to break the news as painlessly as possible.

Now, with Dani up there "truly thinking" among the monsters, the least he could do was to try for a cheerful note. Quickly he got out his wallet to use as a flat surface to write on, squatted down to use a knee for a desk, and began scribbling on the reverse side of her note.

"I wasn't sad," he wrote. "It was a pain in the stomach." After a pause for thought he added, "But I'm glad you're *thinking. Now* can I go to bed?"

Unable to remember the French equivalent of "sweet dreams" or anything along that line, he merely concluded, "Until tomorrow. Mike." Then, folding the note as he went, he returned to the recess at the base of the buttress, fastened the note to the string, and gave three quick jerks on the line.

Dani must have been holding the twine in her hand because it began to move instantly and the note was on its way up to the tower. Michael stood up, watching the scrap of white make its ascent. His eye followed it as it rose past his head, the iron nut making a tiny scraping sound against the stones, and on up. . .

"Venez-y! Faîtes vite!"

The sharp, authoritative voice cracked like a rifleshot

and seemed to lift Michael off his feet and flip him around, his back to the cathedral wall, face toward the figure that loomed against the light at its back. The man wore the unmistakable short cape and round hat, and his right arm was making imperative come-here motions to supplement his spoken commands. He wasn't a particularly big police-man, but he was certainly a lot bigger than Michael, and he blocked the only way out of this stone trap.

Michael's reaction, like the sneeze in the bell tower, amazed him by its lightning speed—but not until much later when he had time to think about it. Though his body seemed to move with the speed of sound, his brain outdid the speed of light. In spite of all that assortment of velo-cities it didn't occur to him that he had nothing to fear from the police. He had broken no law, nor was he about to break one. All he thought of was that highly visible little rectangle of paper so jerkily ascending the side of the cathedral just above his head. Let this policeman so much as glance toward it and the game was over for Dani, and it would be Michael's fault.

There was only one thing to do: He must at whatever cost prevent the policeman from looking up. With no fur-ther thought, he dug his toes into the paving blocks and launched himself like a projectile at the open space be-neath the officer's gesturing arm.

In the time it would ordinarily take to blink in a leisure-ly manner a tremendous number of things happened. The swinging cape went *flap* against his face, a startled Gallic oath sounded loud in his ear, the gesturing arm dealt him a glancing blow as it tried to clamp down on his catapulting body, shoes shuffled loudly on stone as the man pivoted on his right foot to bring his other arm into action, and a set of iron fingers clawed their way down the back of

Michael's neck, caught at the neckline of his tight-fitting T-shirt, then dropped away. Michael was free and running like a deer with the hounds on its trail.

Only because he turned out to be pointed in that direction, he ran along the south side of Notre Dame, between it and the two small buildings that flanked it near the river's edge. If he kept on in a straight line, he would pass beyond the rear of the cathedral through a line of trees at the south edge of an open square. At the end of the square was the short street which led across the tip of the island from the Bridge of the Archbishopric. Where this street turned westward and became the Quai aux Fleurs, a footbridge angled off to the right, crossing the narrow stretch of river dividing this island from the neighboring Île St. Louis.

He knew that it would be an excellent idea to get off the island he was on just as quickly as possible. The police, if they were so inclined, could easily seal it off from the rest of the city and hunt a person down at their leisure.

So, if he was to get off this island, he had to do one of three things: He could run straight on to the street that lay ahead, make a right turn, and cross the Pont de l'Archevêché to the Left Bank and make his way home from there by the most direct route. He could double back, going all the way around the cathedral to his left or around the palace of the archbishop to his right, coming out in either case on the Rue d'Arcole and crossing back over the Pont Double the way he had come. Or he could angle leftward across the open square and cross the footbridge to the Île St. Louis, where other possibilities would then be open to him.

All these twisting and turning tactics of evasion shot through his mind while his feet went on doing their thing at peak efficiency. Even before he had reached the rear of the cathedral, the sound of heavy shoes pounding on pavement behind him halted abruptly, and in its place came the shrill, penetrating tweet of a whistle, thrice repeated.

Almost before this somehow chilling sound was swallowed up by the other sounds of the city, it was echoed—not from behind him, but from somewhere ahead and perhaps a little to the right. A signal, and a reply? There seemed little doubt about it. Michael veered away from danger—the second sound, which must have come from the point where the bridge ahead of him reached the island. When he reached the edge of the square behind the cathedral, he was aimed toward the footbridge, but he didn't move diagonally across the square; instead he dodged left, then right, keeping instinctively to the shadow of the trees that lined it. As he zigzagged, there was the sound of another whistle, but he couldn't place it. By this time his lungs were laboring like a leaky bellows, and it occurred to him how pleasant it would be to slow down at least to a trot. That was impossible, of course, unless he wanted to get caught, in which case there was no point in having run in the first place. He did pause, however, when his flying feet brought him to the very end of a row of trees at the northern edge of the square. Now he had no choice but to move into the open and cross the footbridge. He eyed it with misgiving, trying to use the brief pause to get his breathing under control. He could see a few people moving across the bridge, in either direction. None of them, at least from this distance, looked like a policeman.

From somewhere—behind him and to the north, it seemed—came the sound of another whistle, and he actually had had a moment in which to jeer at himself for the feeling of importance it gave him. Maybe they actually

were sealing off the whole Île de la Cité (with whistles—
and shortwave radio too, of course) just on account of
him. Michael "Magic Fingers" Horner, international jewel
thief, wanted by the police on two continents. Make it
three.

Go across the bridge, he told himself disgustedly. Just
go across the bridge!

He started across—strolling, hands in pockets, the very
picture of carefree boyhood and innocent intentions, the
back of his neck crawling slightly at the thought of batteries of official eyes watching his every move. About halfway across the bridge a new thought struck him—one that
should have struck him before and would have if he hadn't
been in such a panic. The Île St. Louis was where Uncle
Fernand lived!   And where Uncle Fernand lived there
might be platoons of policemen and acres of detectives on
the lookout for the kidnappers of Danielle de la Tour.
While none of these minions of the law would be looking,
in all probability, for a thirteen-year-old kidnapper, they
just *might* be looking for a thirteen-year-old assistant kidnapper—a lookout, spy, messenger boy, something of the
sort. And here he was, heading right into their clutches.

He reached the other end of the bridge, however, and
nobody clutched. No Parisian sheriff's posse lurked. There
was merely a large intersection, not very well populated at
the moment, with massive apartment buildings rising above
it and the usual café on each corner.

Michael quickly turned his mind to what his next move
should be. Whether or not the police were sealing off the
Île de la Cité as he had imagined, there was no doubt about
those whistles and certainly none about the cop from
whom he had escaped. Even though he was guilty of
nothing worse than fleeing from a policeman, it wouldn't

do to be caught if he could help it. They would question him, and no telling what they might find out. Suddenly he thought of the detective on the tower, the one with the sub-zero eyes. He shuddered. That man could probably get information out of a brick. No, thank you all the same, Michael didn't care to be questioned.

So what was the next move? It seemed obvious. So far he had accomplished nothing but to get from one island to another, and if one island could be sealed off, so could the next. The smart move, then, was to get off this one too, by the shortest route possible, and to do that, he had only to follow his nose. The short street on which he now found himself led straight to a vehicular bridge which crossed to the Right Bank. Even though it meant that every step was taking him farther away from home, he headed for the bridge. On the way he met a few strollers and passed others. None paid any attention to him. The clods! Little did they know that Magic Fingers Horner was passing among them, making another getaway that in time would become the talk of the underworld! On four continents.

At the far end of the bridge he paused to look around for some sort of bearing. He had never been in this particular section of Paris before, a fact which wouldn't have troubled him at all in ordinary times, so accustomed had he become to finding his way around in this huge metropolis. But right now there was more urgency than usual. The object was to get home as quickly as possible without setting foot on either of the islands. On foot this would mean a tremendously long detour, either upstream or down, and get him home so late it would be impossible to explain what he'd been up to.

There were cabs, of course, but cab riding was a luxury frowned upon in the Horner household. Besides, he had read enough detective stories to know that the police were always finding out about people by questioning cabdrivers.

So that left—well, of *course*—how dumb could he get?—the metro! The *métropolitain*. On this fast, efficient subway system you could go anywhere in Paris. One line, which he had ridden often, went right underneath the Seine and the Île de la Cité, with a station at the Place St. Michel, a mere skip and a jump from home. Somewhere around here there was bound to be a station and another line to connect with that one. So what was he waiting for?

He was standing at an intersection, facing a treelined boulevard on the far side of which were the lights of cafés and shops. The thing to do was go over there and ask where the nearest metro station was.

He crossed the boulevard, which a sign informed him was the Quai de l'Hôtel de Ville, passed through a small square, crossed another street and was making for the entrance to the nearest café when its doors opened and two solid figures emerged. They wore round blue hats, short blue capes, and fierce mustaches. They were looking Michael straight in the eyes. One policeman for each eye.

Actually, as it turned out, they were looking straight in the eye of iron-nerved Magic Fingers Horner, who smiled a smile that looked pleasant but felt sick and said, "*S'il vous plaît, messieurs—où se trouve la station du métro la plus proche?*" (If it you pleases, my sirs, where finds itself the metro station the most near?) Magic Fingers spoke excellent French.

One of the policemen raised one hand and pointed down the street to Michael's left. "*Là-bas,*" he said.

Michael looked, and sure enough, *là-bas* it was—the familiar illuminated blue-and-red sign of the metro.

"*Merci, m'sieu,*" he said with profound gratitude and immeasurable relief, and within the space of two minutes was vanishing into the bowels of the Parisian earth.

Not quite fifteen minutes later he was climbing yet again the stairway to the apartment—very wearily this time. It had been a long, long day. Outside the door he paused to look at his watch to see just how long a day it really had been. The watch said nine fifty-five and he looked a second time in disbelief. It *couldn't* have been a mere hour and five minutes since he had gone *down* these stairs! He even held the watch to his ear to make sure it was running, and as he did so, he heard his mother's voice, then his father's. He couldn't make out what they said but could tell they were both in the living room. Waiting for him, maybe?

Then, just as he was putting his hand on the doorknob a third voice spoke. It was a man's voice, deep and resonant. The man was speaking English with an accent, but there was no mistaking what he said.

"He will have many questions to answer—your son. It will be necessary that he tell all."

The time of day stopped mattering, Magic Fingers Horner vanished like a wisp of smoke in a hurricane, and Michael stood in the dimly lighted hallway, listening to the voice of doom.

It was incredible, but it had happened. With almost nothing to go on they had found out who he was and traced him here. They were superhumanly clever. His first impulse was to turn and steal quickly down the stairs again. Surely there was some place he could hide—and if they couldn't find him, they couldn't question him—and if they couldn't question him, they couldn't find out about Dani. . . . He felt his shoulders sag, knowing it wouldn't work. Even if he could hide out somewhere, it wouldn't be fair to Mom and Dad, who would worry themselves sick. And anyway, if the police were all that clever, they'd soon find him. No, there was nothing to do now but go in there—face the music—get it over with. Taking a very deep breath, he opened the door and walked in on legs that felt as stiff as fence posts.

There had been sound and at least a little movement in the living room the instant before his entrance, but now it all came to a stop, and five pairs of eyes zeroed in on Michael's face. Three of them belonged to his family— Mom and Lucinda in chairs by the fireplace, Dad leaning against the frame of the door to the balcony. The fourth belonged to the very large, very blond young man who was sitting bolt upright on the sofa that would become Michael's bed—if bedtime ever came again. The fifth (and here the picture began to go awry) were those of an extremely pretty dark-haired young woman who sat beside the man. His wife? But that was crazy; no detectives, even French ones, brought their wives along when they were working. Neither did detectives suddenly break out with a smile and surge to their feet with an enormous hand outstretched toward the person from whom they were about to pry the innermost secrets.

Then Dad smiled too. "Mike," he said, "come and meet your substitute parents—Dr. and Mrs. Muller!"

The only thing, Michael felt sure, that kept him from collapsing to the floor was the fact that his right hand was grasped, practically up to the armpit, and shaken with a violence of enthusiasm that threatened to loosen his teeth. The powerful voice engulfed him. "A-*ha!* Ze yoong Michael! What plesshures for me, for my wife! To your fater have I already apple-o-jice. Now again to you must I apple-o-jice for so late the intrusion. But today I have obtain the tickets to America, to Portlandoregon—and I am so filled with excitements that I must come and tell and make the agwaintance of you." He beamed down at Michael, so crammed with goodwill that even as vast an acreage of skin as his could not contain it all.

With a quick but dazzling smile for Michael and a ferocious frown for her husband, the pretty Mrs. Muller said, "Franz! Please to stop *mauling* poor Michael! If you do not stop, we will have no guide to America—and Professor Horner will throw you down the stairs!"

Everybody laughed at the thought of this giant being hurled down the stairs by angular Professor Horner. Everybody, that is, but Michael, who was caught by a feeling of panic. Everything, moving much too fast for him, was getting completely out of control.

All the heavy thinking that had been his excuse for going out in the first place had remained undone. Instead of arriving at decisions, he had been fleeing from policemen.

The genial student of volcanoes gave Michael's arm back to him miraculously unfractured and apple-o-jiced again. "Here in Europe," he said, "I am a big man. In your country I will be a midget. I will be—how say you—I will be *tenderfeet!* That is why you must tell all to me—how to go here, how to go there, when to arise of a morning, how to buy bread. *Everysing* to me you must tell!"

With that the spate of words dried up abruptly. The giant clasped his arms behind his back and stood rocking forward and backward and beaming down at Michael as if he asked no more of life than to go on admiring him forever.

Until that moment there had been no need for Michael to say anything at all, and no chance. Now there was. He could feel all those eyes on him, hear the ears listening, and his brain was miles from catching up with itself. If only everything didn't have to come *at* him so fast! He felt like a lion set upon by hounds. Small lion. Big hounds.

He didn't know what to do, what to say—but he had to do and say *something*. He lifted agonized eyes to those of his father, clear across the room, and said in a voice unrecognizable as his own, "I'm not going—I've got to stay here."

16

The Absolute Truth

Many times in his life Michael had had reason to marvel at his father's ability to stay cool when everybody else was coming to a boil. "Your father," as Mom sometimes put it, "is always flying into a calm."

He flew into one now, probably in response to all the agony in his son's eyes. The results were little short of miraculous. In the space of only a few minutes the volcanologist and his wife, a bit bewildered but still ecstatic, had been sped on their way with assurances that a welcome still awaited them in Oregon, with or without the son of the house of Horner; Mom had been skillfully diverted from her expressed intention to get right to the bottom of Michael's incomprehensible behavior; Lucinda, after being shushed repeatedly, had been coerced into going to her room.

As for Michael, he was invited to get into his pajamas and then split a bottle of sody-pop with Dad. Mom glared at Dad, only half in fun. "Do I take it," she asked icily, "that I am not invited to this—this *carousal?*"

Dad looked apologetic. "Well, maybe you could go bead a moccasin or something."

"Moccasin be hanged! I'll—" This time Mom couldn't keep the light touch going and after a moment she left the room, giving Michael an uncertain, apprehensive sort of smile.

He felt more than a little apprehensive himself as he got into his pajamas and waited for Dad to come with the drinks. The most uncomfortable part of it all was the knowledge that whatever was about to happen to him would be no more than he deserved. After all the com-motion he had made about going home, and all the trouble Dad had gone to, making it possible for him to do it, what did *he* do? He got all soft in the head about a girl and upset the applecart. The worst of it was that he couldn't explain why— not without giving away a secret that wasn't his to give. And an explanation, of course, would be the first thing Dad would ask for.

He should have known better; Dad almost never did what a person expected him to do. What he said after he had brought the drinks and settled himself in the chair opposite Michael's couch didn't have a thing in the world to do with an explanation.

"You know, Mike," he said, rattling the ice in his glass and peering into it, "being a parent is the toughest job a person ever has. And everybody who is one is expected to be good at it." He smiled an absentminded, rueful smile.

"But there's no school—no college—you can go to and learn how. So what happens? You make mistakes."

He paused to sip his drink while Michael poised himself warily for what would come next, then continued. "With the best will in the world you make mistakes. I do. Your mother does. But we're in it together, and we can maybe correct each other—balance each other—cancel out a mistake here and there.

"But what if she weren't around—if something should happen to her? A man thinks about that sometimes. Well, being a parent then would be *more* than twice as tough. I'd make *more* than twice as many mistakes. And when you make a mistake as a parent it can last a lifetime—the lifetime of another human being."

Again he paused and this time caught Michael by surprise with a sudden grin. "Now don't turn yourself off— you'll see what I'm driving at in a minute. Anyway, it occurred to me recently—*very* recently—to consider what it might be like if I were single—a bachelor with no thought of being anything *but* a bachelor—and all of a sudden, almost overnight, I were to become a parent."

Michael must have been looking as blank as he was feeling because Dad added in explanation, "A foster parent—a guardian. Suppose my brother and his wife were to be killed, in an accident, and I suddenly found myself in charge of a—a girl, let's say—about your age."

The thing that went *boing* inside Michael's head must have been visible in his face; otherwise there was no accounting for Dad's concentrated manner of not looking at him. What Dad had just said—or rather *almost* said—was impossible. He *couldn't* know everything he seemed to be saying he knew. Michael must be imagining it. In just a moment now Dad would say something to prove he wasn't

superhuman either, that he couldn't and didn't know that
Michael had anything to do with Danielle de la Tour and
her uncle.

"Now it's just as natural for me to see things from the
uncle's point of view," Dad said, "as it is for you to see
them from the girl's."

So much for prognostication. Michael Horner, father
forecaster.

"And what I see is a man who's probably—tonight, right
now—going back for the thousandth time over all the
mistakes he's made and suffering like the damned for every
one of them."

For a few moments the silence was as deep as silence
ever can be in a huge city. The rush of traffic along the
quay was stilled for a time, held by the traffic light up at
the Place du Petit Pont. Down on the river a barge gave a
doleful hoot. Michael, strung as tight as a bowstring, felt
incapable of either sound or movement.

Dad went on. "It's all guesswork, Mike. Maybe I'm
multiplying two by two and getting seven. Maybe he's a
monster, this uncle, and would as soon be rid of the niece
as not. Maybe to him she's—as you put it—just a pain in
the neck. . . ."

So there was confirmation of what Michael had feared
all along. Maybe Dad wasn't superhuman, but he was
certainly a superthinker. And, naturally, it was Michael
himself who had set the thinking process in motion. If
only he'd said nothing at the proper time—But no, he'd
had to sound off about it, make noises about how rotten
Uncle Fernand was—and that, of course, set Dad off.

Michael was so busy rethinking his father's supposed
thoughts that it took him a moment to catch up with his
actual words, which had scarcely paused. "Terrified. That
would be my reaction—plain, unvarnished panic. Here I

am, a middle-aged bachelor whose talents run to big business, not to matrimony and parenthood, and out of a clear sky I'm a father. And I'm not the father of a little baby that I can get used to bit by bit. I'm the father of a nearly grown girl who—if that picture in the paper tells a true story—would be quite a handful even for her real father."

In spite of everything, Michael had to think a secret smile as he considered Dad's words. It was true beyond doubt that Dani de la Tour would be quite a handful.

"So what I would do," Dad went on with a considering air, as if he had given the matter a great deal of thought, "would be to resolve to do my best to take the place of a father and mother—and my best would be pretty awful. I'd make clumsy overtures because I wouldn't know how to make deft ones. She would reject them because she'd have no way of understanding the spirit in which they were meant. And so it would go, from bad to worse, and maybe at last I'd just give up and hire somebody—a companion, governess, somebody like that—and provide whatever money was needed, and hope for the best."

Dad's pause this time lasted so long that Michael thought he had finished, but then he smiled an odd little half-smile and added, "Chances are I'd be getting fond of this child but not daring to let it show, which to her would make me seem more indifferent than ever, and—" Now he smiled ruefully and shrugged. "That's what people do, Mike; they get themselves into little boxes they can't get out of, even though there may be a perfectly easy way. Like birds. You've seen them. They fly into a building through an open door and can't get out again unless somebody helps them, even though the door's still open."

After that, without any warning, he got to his feet and stood looking down at Michael and rattling what little ice was left in his glass. "And that," he said, "is the end of the arithmetic exercise. Two times two equals two hundred and twenty-two." He reached for Michael's glass. "Finished?"

Michael nodded, handing the glass up. But he waited, watchfully. This couldn't be the end of anything.

Again he was wrong. "Well," Dad said, "guess I'll go crawl in the sack, too. Want me to turn off your light?"

Michael stared up at him. This just couldn't be happening. "You mean—" His voice sounded strange, probably because he hadn't been using it much lately. "You mean you're not going to ask me how come I all of a sudden don't want to go home?"

Dad grinned. "If I did ask you, what would you tell me—the truth?"

"Well. . . not exactly." This considered reply sounded so peculiar that Michael had to answer Dad's grin with one of his own.

"That's why I'm not going to ask you. Can't go encouraging my son to trifle with the truth. And anyway, Mike—"

"Uh—yes?"

"If you did—trifle with the truth, I mean—I'd have a pretty good notion you were doing it to help somebody else. And now"—his tone became matter-of-fact—"now I'm going to give your poor mother a break and let her come say good-night to you."

Mom had come and gone, the warmth of her presence lingering in the now-darkened room. "Dad made me promise," she had said just before kissing him good-night, "that I wouldn't ask you what this is all about—and I won't. But there's nothing to stop me from guessing—except that everything I guess is more worrisome than the last thing."

He had most solemnly assured her there was nothing to worry about. "I'd tell you in a minute," he said, "only I sort of made a promise myself."

Now he was alone, and it was very late. The city sounds were quieting down to their after-midnight murmur, the filmy white curtains at the balcony door were swaying ghostlike in the gentle breeze that entered along with the faint illumination from the street below, and Michael's couch was enormously welcoming, though lumpy.

But his eyes stubbornly refused to stay shut. It had been a day too full of thumps and jolts and jabs and wrenches to let sleep take over without a struggle. Otherwise he would have been dead to the world when Lucinda came to call. Her bare feet went shuffle-pat on the tiles in the little hallway and then hush-hush across the warm rug. "Mike," she whispered, after a long and listening pause, "are you asleep?"

"Yes," replied Michael, also whispering.

"Oh, good. I was afraid you really might be."

"Fat chance!" He hoped he sounded put-upon. Actually, tired or not, there was something to be said for being the center of so much attention. It was impossible to believe that only a few days ago his family and the world at large had seemed bent upon erasing him altogether.

"Mike"—Lucinda sat down precariously on the edge of his couch, and he slid over automatically to make room—"I won't ask you a lot of questions. I won't ask you *any* questions. But I can't go to sleep until you tell me if I'm right about just *one* thing. Will you?"

"Well, *I* don't know. Ask me!"

"I will—but you've got to swear to tell the absolute truth."

Michael took a little time to think this over. It sounded

like a trap. "Okay," he said finally, "I'll either tell the absolute truth or I won't answer at all. Now ask the question."

"You'll tell the truth even if it embarrasses you—makes you feel silly?"

"Okay—okay!"

"Because there's no reason it *should* make you feel silly. After all, it's the most natural thing in the world, and—"

"For gosh *sake*, Cindy, are you going to ask me or—"

"And it's the only *possible* reason you'd turn down the chance to—"

"Go *on!* Ask your *question!*"

"Michael"—her voice, in spite of being only a whisper, managed to convey a sense of excitement, an invitation to the sharing of confidences at her age level instead of his own—"Michael, have you got a girl?"

His response was as automatic as scratching an itch. "Well, for gosh sake—what a dumb question! Of *course* I haven't got a— How could I have a—"

"The truth, Michael, the absolute truth!"

He squirmed, scowling into the darkness. What *was* the absolute truth? At home, to "have a girl" meant you paid special attention to a certain girl, teased her more than others, maybe, and let it be known among the other boys, without actually saying so, that she was your girl. Maybe you managed to sit just across the aisle from her in the school bus or at the same table in the cafeteria. Things like that. If that was what it meant to have a girl, then it had nothing to do with Dani de la Tour.

But if it meant that a face kept popping in front of your mind's eye all unbidden, if the sound of a voice kept getting between you and other sounds, and the face and voice belonged to a girl who—well—*bothered* you more than any other girl ever had, a girl who could make you feel good all over when she laughed and downright miserable when she looked unhappy, a girl it was more comfortable to be with than to be away from, a girl who—

"Yeah," he said with gruff inelegance, looking up at his sister, whose face was a whitish oval framed softly by dark hair. "Yeah, I guess you could say I've got a girl."

"I knew it!" she said. "I just *knew* it!" It was the first time Michael had ever *heard* somebody smile. "Oh, Mike, I think it's just wonderful!" Her whisper escalated into a low tone, all throaty and dramatic. "Just think! Paris in the spring—your first love—a French girl—"

"Hey, wait a minute! Are you off your. . . you think I'm going to get *married* or something?"

"Of *course* not, Mike," she said with a touch of impatience. "Not *now*. But who knows? Maybe the years will pass, and you'll never quite forget each other. You'll write letters. And then someday you'll come back to Paris and she'll be waiting, and—"

"Maybe so," Michael interrupted, grinning into the darkness where it wouldn't show. Lucinda was enjoying herself so much he hated to spoil it. "But I'll never live that long if I don't get some sleep."

A little later, after she had gone shuffle-patting back to her room, taking her audible smile along, and when sleep was about to pounce at last, he had a premonition. Not a grand and memorable premonition about wars and floods and other cataclysms. Just a down-at-heel, shiny-pants sort of premonition which told him out of the corner of its mouth that if he thought *today* had been rough, just wait till he got a load of *tomorrow*.

17

The Magic Circle

The thing to do, Michael told himself as he plodded up the north tower's spiral stair the next morning, was to act as if nothing had changed between yesterday and today. Just play it cool. Forget everything Lucinda had said—and darn Lucinda anyway! Just be casual, matter-of-fact. Deadpan Horner.

So far this morning nothing had happened to bear out his premonition of the night before. On the contrary, the day had begun in a very relaxing sort of way. He had awakened to find himself the sole occupant of the apartment, the others having gone their several ways. Obviously they had gone to considerable trouble to let him sleep. For this he was grateful—not because he felt he needed the extra sleep but because it spared him the necessity of being confronted—but it also made him uneasy, thinking how it must have been achieved. The three of them tiptoeing around shushing one another and talking about him in stage whispers. His ears burned when he thought of it, but still it could have been worse. Thanks to a funny note Mom had left under the cereal box he knew at least that neither Dad nor Cindy had shared what each knew secretly.

"Mike," she had written, "Eat anything right side middle shelf fridge. (Except containers.) If you do anything to get arrested, deported, or executed, please send postcard. P.S. Everybody in this family knows something except your mother. Nobody ever tells mothers anything. Every day is father's day. Don't ever be a mother. Love. Mother."

Immediately upon reading this message, he resolved that when and if it should ever become possible to tell all about the state of affairs he was now tangled up in, the first person to hear about it would be Mom.

This morning he had equipped himself with sketchbook and pencils in order to take up his role as the dedicated gargoyle sketcher. Just before leaving the apartment he had added to his burden a small album of photographs he had taken here and there around home, plus a few scenic Oregon postcards. The Horner propaganda machine was about to go into action, though not with very high hopes on the part of its principal propagandist. He had also put on his father's goggle-type dark glasses, though he told himself scornfully that it was a pretty sorry excuse for a disguise.

It made him *feel* incognito anyway, and he took the further feeble precaution of approaching the cathedral from a slightly different direction. He knew it was silly, but he felt a crawling at the back of his neck at the thought of passing the base of the south tower where the policeman had cornered him. To avoid it, he crossed to the island on the Petit Pont and strolled diagonally across the Parvis, arriving at the entrance to the north tower stairs just as the door was thrown open to admit the usual jostling knot of tourists. About half of them were children ranging down to five or six years old, which was a good thing because they could be counted on to distract their elders from whatever anybody else might be doing. Better still, they spoke an assortment of languages he didn't understand, leaving him free to pay his two francs and doggedly climb the scooped-out steps and tell himself over and over again that the thing to do was play it cool, forget about Lucinda, be casual. . . . But thanks to Dad and Cindy—and of course, to his unreliable self—he felt about as cool as a potato getting itself french-fried.

The first thing he did as he emerged into the light from the spiral of stone was to turn for a look at Charly. This was surprising because he hadn't been consciously thinking about Charly. But there he was—ugly and stupid and crammed to his beetle brows with good intentions. He's like me, Michael thought—leaning there thinking and thinking and thinking but not getting anywhere because he hasn't got much to think with. For a minute Michael allowed himself the luxury of envy. How relaxing it would be to be Charly. Just to lean there and admire the scenery and never to get hungry or tired, or cold, or worried or afraid. Nobody expecting you to say anything clever, or solve any problems, make decisions, do anything useful at all. . .

With a sigh Michael tore himself loose from Charly's

subversive spell and made his way along the balustrade to the inner corner of the south tower where crouched below the monster with the sharply jutting elbows. Here he opened his sketchbook on the broad stone railing and began a drawing of Old Elbows' nearest neighbor, the chimera who guarded the outer corner of this balcony. This one was an almost-human monster and therefore one of the scariest of all, with a man's torso and a subhuman, apelike head.

There were others he would have preferred to draw, but this one put him in the best position for a quick scramble between Old Elbows and the iron barrier when the proper time came. His principal concern at this point was the *gardien* who could appear from around a corner at any moment, and nearsighted or not, he could scarcely fail to see a moving figure in a place where a figure shouldn't be. Thanks to luck it hadn't happened yesterday, but the time had come when it would be smart to substitute caution for luck. He would wait until the *gardien* had led a group into the bell tower. Meanwhile, there was the drawing to do.

Under the circumstances it was no surprise that it didn't go well at first, that he had to chew his tongue a lot and make frequent erasures, but minutes went by, and more minutes, and soon he had forgotten everything else. The result was that the monster began to take very creditable shape on the paper, and Michael was actually beginning to admire his handiwork when the spell was broken by the penetrating voice of the *gardien* making itself heard above the babble of the tourists. *"Suivez-moi, mesdames, messieurs!"*

Michael bent even more industriously over the sketchbook and refrained from looking around at the official as, keys jangling, he led his first tour party of the day toward the black metal door of the bell gallery. Unobtrusively Michael pocketed his pencil and eraser and closed the book, doing his best at the same time to twitch his ears backward, like a horse. The tone of voice altered as the man stepped inside. The other voices, chirruping with anticipation, followed, and in a moment all were muted as the door swung shut. Michael bent down swiftly, shoved the book and album under the grille, straightened, swept all visible sides of the parapet with a glance. For an instant he was alone, and in that instant he scrambled like a monkey between Old Elbows and the grille, dropped to the other side, scooped up the books again, and scuttled lizardlike around the corner.

After that he was free to follow the zigs and zags that led to the eastern side of the tower, home of the prettiest gargoyle.

As he made his final zag he came to a startled halt. Light as a tumbleweed, the form of the prettiest gargoyle, encased in a black leotard, was spinning toward him along the parapet in a series of lightning step turns, the feathery grace of her movements hampered only slightly by the little radio clutched in one hand. The sound of the music came and went in the same fast rhythm with which her face appeared, disappeared, and reappeared.

He could tell the instant at which she caught sight of him, for a smile lighted up her face. Her dark eyes were already aglow with the joy of movement. But she didn't stop. Waving a quick greeting as she approached, she quickly reversed direction and went spinning off again to the other end of the balustrade. There, apparently, the music reached a conclusion, and she sank to the stone floor in one of those deep curtsies Michael had always crassly referred to as the "dying-duck slump" back in

Lucinda's ballet days. There was nothing ducklike in the way Dani did it, though; it was more like a silky pinwheel of thistledown coming gently to rest on a bed of moss.

Appalled at himself for giving headroom to so fancy a flight, he eyed the leotard and ballet slippers grumpily. "What have you got up here—a whole durn wardrobe?"

She rose with her characteristic effortlessness and stumped toward him with the graceless gait of all ballerinas walking flatfooted on toe shoes. "Holdern?" she mimicked. "I do not know this 'holdern.' "

He had to grin, but the grin began quickly to feel strained, because her eyes seemed to be roving over his face, probing—and for all he knew seeing—what ought to remain hidden. Then she too grinned companionably, almost as if she knew he needed to be put at ease. "Good morning, Michael Horner," she said, "and how is your so-disturbed digestion this morning?"

"Digestion?" Then he remembered the note he had written the night before. "I cured it," he said, "by running away from a policeman."

Now he had her complete attention and was proceeding to make the most of it when she broke in excitedly. "I knew! I knew that something was not right. I read your so funny note and I watch." She gestured toward Old Longview lying on top of the rolled-up sleeping bag. "I watch, and you do not come to your window. But your father comes and he looks up and down the street, and I tell myself, 'He looks for Mike—he has fear for him.' Then another man comes—a huge man— a whole *Alp* of a man— and *he* looks for Mike. Who is this man?"

Coming as it did, hot on the heels of her quoted dialogue with herself, the question didn't sound at first as if it were meant for him, and he fumbled. "Oh—him. He's the man who—he's—just a man my father knows." Skittering thus around the edge of this pitfall, he finished telling the story of his flight from the law. It would cause no end of complications for Dani to find out where Dr. Muller fitted into the picture.

His story finished, he eased himself down on the ledge beside the sleeping bag and after fiddling around for a time with the telescope and its focusing ring he said, "You know, I've been thinking. . . . "

She sat down beside him, silent but receptive, removed the slippers and wiggled her toes. They both contemplated the wiggling toes for a while, then Dani nodded. "I too have been thinking."

"About going to San Francisco?"

There was a tiny pause. "That—and many other things. But first, you must tell me your thoughts."

"Okay. But I'm like you—there's all sorts of things." He thought about all those things—none of them easy to put into words, some perhaps impossible. But he had to start somewhere. "Since I saw you yesterday," he began, "an awful lot has happened to me."

She nodded emphatically. "With me it has been the same."

"It—it has?" He turned to look at her in surprise. could have happened to her all alone up here? Then he thought he understood. "Oh—something on the radio?"

"No-no. Not the radio. Not anything you would ever guess. But we are not speaking of me. Please to continue."

He glanced at her small, composed profile with an odd feeling of uncertainty. Sometimes she could make him feel she was a whole generation older than he, sometimes just the opposite. "Okay," he said again, and plunged in. "Last night, after I left here and went home, my father and I had a long talk—two long talks. They were about—about very important things."

A sharp exclamation in French made him turn to find her eyes on his face, wide and searching. "It is so very strange! I, too, last night talked—with my father!"

"You—you did?"

The fingers of one hand tapped her forehead. "In my head, of course. He was very much with me—and my mother too—because of what I will tell you." She drew her bare legs up and crossed them, kindergarten fashion, leaned her elbows on her knees, and propped her chin with both fists. "But now Danielle will truly close the mouth. She will *listen*. You spoke with your father—about important matters."

"Well, important to me, anyway." Michael peered abstractedly toward the ornate spire that soared upward from the roof of Notre Dame's great cross. "It's hard to believe," he began, "but if my father hadn't run out of Lifesavers the other day, I'd have gone my whole life without ever knowing there was such a person as you. . . ."

But this was dangerous ground and he hurried on, telling about his discovery of what the gargoyles were for and everything Dad had said as a result. Finishing, he sat silent as wonder grew in him. Then he added, "Gee—I thought—sitting up here in broad daylight and telling about all that, it would sound—you know—silly."

"No-no-no-no!" He turned, startled, to see that she looked almost angry. "No—you must not speak such a word! It is all true—you will be an architect and build beautiful things!" With both hands she patted the weatherworn masonry in front of her crossed legs. "Notre Dame has done this for you! Our Lady—Our Lady of Paris has done it!"

More than a little abashed, Michael said falteringly, "Are you—are you religious?"

Dani shook her head impatiently. "It is not a thing of religious or of not religious, it is a thing of truth. It is the *église*—this church—this cathedral. She does miracles. For hundreds of years she has done them. Mam'selle has spoken of this many times, on our walks, but until last night I did not truly understand. She says—Mam'selle—that Notre Dame does not *make* the miracles but that the miracles are inside people, and Notre Dame"— she struggled visibly to voice so deep a thought in a language not her own—"Notre Dame makes them to—to come forth—to be born!

"And she is right—Mam'selle. Look at *you*, Michael. From out of *you* now she has brought the miracle. And perhaps too from me! Last night I—" She clapped both hands over her mouth. "*Tais-toi*, Dani! Shut you the mouth! You must please to continue, Mike—you had *two* talks with your father, and you have told only the one."

Michael stared at her, feeling cloddish and stupid. It was very hard to tear loose from her impassioned spell and go on. "Well," he said, floundering, "well—the second one was a lot later, after I escaped from the policeman and all that."

This time she listened in silence, broken only once. That was when Michael, nearing the end of his narrative, broke off with a start as the great bell in the tower at his back gave out a single deep-throated note that seemed to strike him just below the breastbone. Dani smiled reassuringly. "The *gardien*. He strikes the bell for the visitors—remember?"

"So anyway," Michael went on, conscious that he was stumbling badly, "it was a case of my father being about as smart as I am dumb. But don't worry, he won't give your secret away. Only he thinks"—now the hard part was coming—"he thinks your uncle is—Dani, remember the other day, first time we talked, when I said you'd be a hard person *not* to get mixed up with?"

With a fleeting smile she nodded, and he went on, "Well, that's what my father thought too—just from seeing your picture in the paper. What he said was you'd be a handful." Seeing her puzzled look, he tried to explain. "I don't know what's French for 'handful.' It means—oh—hard to control, like a—a racehorse."

She laughed aloud but with an obvious effort refrained from saying anything.

"Anyway, to get to the point," Michael went on, feeling dogged about the whole thing, "he thinks you may be wrong about your uncle. He says maybe your uncle is really—well—*fond* of you. Only he doesn't know the right way to show it and does all the wrong things. So then *you* do wrong things and—and there you are—both of you unhappy."

For a time she neither moved nor spoke, and Michael refrained from looking at her, fearing to see hurt or anger in her face. Then she reached into her little pile of belongings, got out the blue stretch pants and a blouse, and put them on, turning her back as she did so. When she turned back to reach down for her sandals, he saw to his immeasurable relief that she was smiling. It was a strange sort of smile, though—"exalted" was the only word that came to his mind, as if she were hearing words, or maybe music, inaudible to him.

Kneeling to fasten the sandals, she again patted the stones beneath her. "It is all of a piece," she said. "Your father too—he is a part of the miracle of Notre Dame." She stood up and turned to the balustrade, laying her arms on the rough stone, facing outward. "And now," she said over her shoulder, "you must finish the story of all that has happened to you."

He got up too, feeling uncertain and oddly diffident. There was a lot he didn't understand, but it didn't seem right to ask questions. "I *am* finished. That's all there is." He leaned on the balustrade beside her and looked down at the side of the cathedral along which he had raced so swiftly the night before. The amazing flying buttresses were below him now, and from here their motion seemed to be downward, like great jets of water spurting out and down from the top of the wall.

His eye was just beginning, more or less on its own initiative, to puzzle away at the secret of how all that tremendous weight of stone could support itself and at the same time support the massive walls of the cathedral, when the prettiest gargoyle put an end to all such speculation. "It is not quite all," she said. "You have not yet told *why* your father had this so late conversation with you."

"Why?" Michael shrugged and determinedly went on looking at the buttresses. "No why to it; he just wanted to talk to me."

Dani, whom he was fast recognizing as an expert at ignoring unimportant remarks, said matter-of-factly, "It had to do with the big man, the Alp who came to see you."

"He came to see my father. I *told* you."

"Yes-yes-yes. You *told* me. But he was waiting for *you*. He came to the balcony to look up and down the street, as I have said. And when at last you came, he was filled with delight. All this have I seen."

"With *my* telescope."

"And after the Alp had spoken, you looked directly at me and—"

"How could I look—" He halted, remembering the magic circle and how Dani had looked straight into his eye.

"And you looked at me with—how do you say—*aux cent coups*"—she finger-fluttered—"with *desperation*, and then—"

Michael felt trapped. "You're a spy! You're a peeping Tom! A peeping Thomasina!"

"And at once the mountain went away, and then your father—"

Michael, more trapped-feeling than ever, burst out, "Gad! Between you and him I might as well put my brain on *television!*"

"Michael, it is not my wish to—to torment you. And if you truly wish that I do not know this thing, then I will not ask more."

"Hah! Maybe you won't ask in so many words—or in any words at all—but you'll *ask*. You'll ask with your left eyebrow. . . or your right elbow. . . or your big toe. Because you know what? You can carry on a whole conversation without ever opening your mouth!"

Having thus cleverly established the fact that he was helpless to conceal anything from her, he was free to tell her what he had secretly wanted her to know all along—namely, that for her sake he had unselfishly sacrificed his chance to do what he had longed to do all these months—go home to Oregon.

So he told her, and it was a heady experience to watch the astonishment, the gratitude, the admiration, and half a dozen other emotions chase one another across her face. But in the end he had to give in, however grudgingly, to the spoilsport honesty he just couldn't help, and as Dani was about to break into voluble speech, he held up a hand like a policeman on a poster and shook his head, frowning ferociously. "Hold everything!" he commanded. "I didn't do it for you—I did it for me. Because—because I *wanted* to. Of course"—he paused, reflecting that this honesty thing had to work both ways: Fair was fair—"of course, right at the time I did it because I couldn't stand the thought of walking out on you. But then I realized—"

Dani interrupted with an uncharacteristic gentleness. "Is it possible still to change your mind—to go home with your Alp after all?"

"I don't know," he replied, considering. "Yes, I suppose I could. But I'm not going to."

She looked away, down along the Seine, and when she turned back, he had a flash of that odd feeling he had had before—that she was suddenly, for a time at least, much, much older than he. "I think," she said, "that now has arrived the time for me to tell you of what occurred last night. It was a happening so—so *impressionnant*—so—*terrifiant*—so—"

"Frightening?" Michael suggested.

"No-no! So *majestueux—solennel—*"

"Awesome, awe-inspiring?"

"*Oui!* Yes! That is it exactly! But come—let us sit over there." She pointed to the balcony at the south end of the walkway. "The sun, it becomes warm, and there the chimeras will shade us. And if you like we will share a"—she smiled fleetingly—"a bottle of sody-pop. It is still chilled, I think, from the night."

18

The Singing Stones

"Never," the prettiest gargoyle began, "can I say properly even in my own language what has occurred. In English"—she shrugged—a shrug of real distress—"in English it will be even *more* impossible. I will make—how do you say? —the *mess* of it. You will say, 'This Dani, she is mad, she is hysterical.'"

"Want to bet?" Michael said sturdily. "You'll tell it in English better than I could." He knew this for the plain truth.

They sat side by side on the stones of the east-facing balcony, with the fretwork of the balustrade cross-hatching their view toward the Île St. Louis and a pair of weatherworn gargoyles fending off the rays of the high-sailing sun. The tall green bottle of *limonade*, from which each of them had taken a ritual sip, stood between them, slightly atilt on the rough stone floor.

"Poorly or well," Dani said, "I must try. And you will understand, Mike, because—because it is a thing we will share, perhaps always. You, and I, and Our Lady of Paris."

She picked up the bottle, took a swallow, and set it down again, after which she cast Mike a sideways look and a wry grimace. "I think that I delay to commence because I am afraid." Then, inflating her chest and making her voice strong, "Very well, then—*alors*—I commence."

"It is last night—after you have run from the police and gone home again. Your Swiss Alp is departed, you have talked with your father, and now your light is extinguished. Pouf! —like a candle—and I am alone. That is so strange, is it not, that I can see a million lights around all Paris, but when your light is gone, I am alone? So I stand here—not just here, but there, around the corner where I face the Seine—and I am holding the little telescope which has now gone blind, and I am feeling strongly the—how do you say? —*la tristesse*."

"Sadness?" Michael said.

"N-n-n-no—sadness is not right. *La tristesse*, it is a—a *happy* sadness. So that is what I feel, a happy sadness, but I do not know why. And then suddenly I see myself and I say, 'Danielle, what craziness is this? It is late. Go to bed!'"

"So I prepare my bed. I lie in it. I say good-night to the gargoyles, I close my eyes—but I do not sleep. This is strange, because I am like the birds: When darkness comes, I sleep. But now it grows later. I do not know how late because though clocks strike, I do not attend and fail to count the hours. The lights go off—the illuminations of the cathedral, you understand—and I make a discovery: The mechanism that turns off the illuminations at the same time turns on the stars. It takes some moments for the eyes to grow accustomed, and then—*voilà!*—the stars!

"I watch the stars and grow almost ready for sleep at last when—slowly, slowly, slowly as a flower opens—I am aware that Notre Dame, this tower, these stones, they are becoming alive. They move beneath my back; they breathe; they sing! And I tell myself this cannot be, that I sleep, I dream! But I know I do not sleep, I do not dream. And then—like the genie from the bottle—my father is with me—here—inside my head. But he is real all the same—as real, Mike, as you are at this moment.

"We are walking, my father and I, along the *tracé*—the track of the railroad. It is in the country, in Provence, where we went long ago in summertime. My father says, 'A train approaches, Dani.' 'But, Papa, I see no train!' I tell him. 'Put your foot on the rail,' he says, 'and you will feel it. Bend down the ear and listen; it will sing to you of its coming.' So I do these things, and he is right; I feel the train, I hear it sing, and I am afraid. 'Papa,' I cry, 'the train will strike us; it will crush us!' And my father laughs and picks me up in his arms, and the fear is gone."

Dani paused. Michael felt her eyes on him, but if she expected him to say something, he had no idea what it could be, so he simply nodded and said, "Go on," in a voice surprisingly hushed. And she went on.

"That is how it began—like the rail that sang. But this time it is not a rail, it is Notre Dame! Now I am truly afraid, for this is a thing which has never before happened, and there is no father here to laugh and hold me.

"I cannot move, I lie as one who is dead. I tremble, but I do not know if it is I, Dani, who trembles or the stones of Notre Dame. But then, soon, I know it is the stones. They tremble more and it seems that the whole earth must shake. Then a sound slowly makes itself known. It is a part of the trembling and it rises, like the wind at first, then like a rush of waters that will rise and rise until they have swallowed the world. . . .

"I cry out. I do not know what I say, but I find that I am out of my bed and on my knees, and it must be a prayer that I cry out because the terrible sound I hear can be nothing but the voice of God!"

Her voice stopped, and Michael, who for some time had been carefully not looking at her for fear of breaking the spell, looked cautiously slantwise to see her sitting bolt upright, hands clenched in front of her, head upturned, her profile as rapt as if she were actually hearing the sounds again and feeling the vibrations. Somehow she managed to transmit to Michael some of the tension that gripped her small body, and his stomach felt tired, as if it had been rigidly braced for a blow. Dani, for her part, looked as if every muscle from face to feet were coiled painfully tight.

Instinctively he did the right thing. With slow movements he picked up the sody-pop and held it out. She turned quickly with a startled smile and took the bottle. As she drank, he could feel her relax almost as if he were doing it himself. After that she leaned back again, embracing her knees, and said almost matter-of-factly, "It was not the voice of God—not truly—except to me only. It was the organ."

"Organ?" repeated Michael, just about as Charly might have said it.

"The organ of the cathedral. You have seen it perhaps—high up by the great rose window. It is an organ huge, enormous, powerful."

Michael had indeed seen it, or at any rate had it pointed out to him. Now he frowned. "But how come—in the middle of the night?"

"It became clear to me," Dani said, "but not until much later, that the organist comes to practice, so that he can be alone with his instrument, and his music—and perhaps with God."

With a shiver Michael nodded, picturing—inaccurately, of course—a misshapen organist who looked like Quasimodo, the Hunchback of Notre Dame, playing away in the pitch-black cathedral in the dead of night.

"But last night," Dani went on, "I did not think of this. I believe I did not truly think at all. The organ, it stole from me the *think* and left only—" She struggled, groping, then shrugged helplessly. "I have no words to say it, not even in French. The sound rose, like the waves of the sea against the shore, until all at once"—she shivered—"up there, in the tower, the *grand bourdon* spoke—the great bell—it spoke its deep, shining, terrible note. . . .

"Afterward, when I am tranquil, I make myself to understand that this is a thing of the sound waves, like the tuning fork which sings when its note is struck on an instrument. The organ spoke the note of the bell, and it answered.

"But all this I do not think at the time of its happening. I think only that Notre Dame—its stones, its towers, its bells—they have come alive, and they speak! Perhaps they speak to others, but I do not know these others; I know only me, Danielle, and they speak to *me*. I am not important enough to be spoken to so. I am a mouse, a worm, a tiny beetle high up on this mountain of stone, but still they speak to me. And whether they speak with the voice of God, or whether they do not, they tell me that I am not

a good person, that I do not make much matter to the
world. That I am not clever and wise and deserving of the
admiration of all. They tell me instead that I am a nothing.
I am a skin stuffed full of vanity and—and of foolishness of
every sort. They say—

She broke off with a quick frown and shake of her head.
"But this too is foolishness and vanity. I talk always too
much of *me*. Now I will tell you only enough to explain
what it is that I must do.

"The time passed—how much time I do not know—and
the music of the organ stopped, and the stones beneath me
turned once more to stones without life, and I lay down
again on my bed. Never have I known such weariness! But
instead of sleep, thoughts came. But I will not tell you of
these thoughts because you have heard already too many.
No, Mike, do not shake your head. However great the
thirst, no one can drink all day. Let it be enough to say
that my father returned to my thoughts, and he was with
me until at last I slept.

"And when I awoke this morning, it seemed that I knew
what I must do—what my father had *told* me I must do.
But I was not sure until you came and told me of *your*
father and all the rest. Then I knew—I *knew*—that everything Mam'selle had told me was true. I knew that Notre
Dame had made a miracle and that now I must go down
from this tower and go home."

For a moment Michael thought that either her accent or
his own ears had played him a trick. "Did you say 'go
home'?" he asked carefully.

She rose to her feet by her usual magical means and
automatically smoothed out a dress she wasn't wearing.
"You have heard correctly, I think," she said. "I must now
go home, to my uncle."

Michael too rose from his seat on the stones, taking his time about it because right now time was what he needed. Time to think. His mind, like the little fish that swallows a bigger one, was busy stretching itself around this strange experience that so plainly had been a shattering one for Dani. He couldn't share it with her, but he had come as close for a few minutes as anyone ever comes to being inside the mind of another, and it made him feel a little shattered.

As she talked, it seemed as though he too felt the vibration of the stones, the crescendo of sound, the voice of the great bell. And he understood how all this would make a person feel helpless, fearful, insignificant, and overwhelmed by remorse for all his wickednesses, large or small. He could understand, too, how one might emerge from such an experience with a high resolve to correct one's shortcomings, to make amends for offenses against others, and to become a better person.

On the other hand, there was a great deal that he didn't understand, for the simple reason that he wasn't Dani de la Tour. Not even she, for all her powers of expression, could tell him what her thoughts of her dead father had been and what they had to do with her uncle and this decision she had made. And even if she could tell him, perhaps she might not choose to. It was, after all, her decision to make, not his. And that decision meant that she was giving up, that she would go to San Francisco with her uncle. (Or he supposed it meant that.) And *that* meant there was a pretty good chance that he and she might get together again. And that was what he had wanted all along, wasn't it? Well, sure, but—But what? Why did he feel that foot-dragging resistance, this vague sense of incompleteness, of dissatisfaction?

"Mike, you are unhappy with me."

He came out of his puzzled questioning to the realization that he had been scowling for some time at one of the many ornate little knobs of stone that decorated the arch of the bell tower behind and above Dani's head and that she was regarding him with an uncertain smile.

He forced a grin which felt so much like a gargoyle's grin that he quickly gave it up as a bad job and shook his head. "No, I'm not unhappy with you. And even if I was, it wouldn't make any difference. You're the one who's got to decide. But—"

"But!" she echoed. "Always there is a 'but.'" Stepping over to the balustrade, she leaned her back against it and cocked an eyebrow at him with a trace of her customary animation. "Very well, tell me, then, this 'but.'"

Needing no more urging, Michael joined her at the railing—facing outward, however, with the idea that the traffic over on the Left Bank would be less distracting than Dani's face. "Okay," he said. "It's just that I don't think you ought to be in such a rush."

"Rush?"

"Hurry. You shouldn't be in such a hurry to give in." As she made another questioning sound, he added quickly, "To give up, quit, surrender."

"But it is not to surrender! It is—for me—a victory! Do you not understand, Mike? Notre Dame tells me—or perhaps it is my father who tells me—that what I have done is wrong, that I must do better, that I must *be* better. And so I try to—to take away the wrong thing and to do better. This is not to surrender!"

"Now that," said Michael, "is more like it!" He turned his conviction growing stronger. "What you've decided to do is at least partly because of what my father said. You told me so. But what if he's wrong? He could be, you know, even if he is right about a lot of things. He was only guessing, after all, about how things were between you and your uncle. Maybe—"

"No, Mike! He was correct, your father! I was not pleasant—I was not *kind* to my uncle. I did not permit him to—"

"Well, all right, but"—Michael's convictions were gaining strength—"but he wasn't just as *kind* as *he* could have been either. You weren't just making it up—just *inventing* it—when you first told me about him. So what I think is that my father was only *part* right. Maybe you were a stinker, but so was your uncle, so—"

A delicate snort interrupted him, and he looked around to see her eyes alive with laughter. "Stinker," she repeated. "That is so funny a word. I like it, I think—to be a stinker."

"Now that," said Michael, "is more like it!" He turned a real grin on her. Now he was getting things back under control again. Michael Horner, master of his fate. "So what we've got here is a situation that calls for a compromise."

"Compromise?"

"Sure. You give a little, and you take a little. Like nations do when they make treaties and things."

"I do not feel," Dani said, "like a very *large* nation. How do we achieve this compromise?"

"Simple." Oddly enough it actually did seem simple, even though he hadn't yet had time to think about it. To gain some time, he proposed that they have a snack, a proposal which Dani accepted with enthusiasm.

While she spread bread liberally with the soft white cheese that Michael referred to as "glurp," he opened another bottle of pop, exercising his mind meanwhile in what he considered an admirably efficient manner. The result, after they were seated on the sleeping bag, bread and cheese in hand, was that he was ready when she threw him a look that nudged.

"All right," he began, "I'll sort of sum things up and tell you my plan. But no interruptions—okay?"

"My mouth," said Dani firmly, "it is locked."

"Okay. Now what you want to do is—"

"But that does not mean I will agree with this plan."

"All right—what you propose to do is just go around the corner there and walk down the stairs and go home. Well, I'll bet you haven't stopped to think how that's going to look. And I don't mean just to your uncle. Don't forget the whole doggone city knows you've either run away or been kidnapped. So if—"

"But it makes no matter what the whole doggone city thinks! Only what *I* think is—"

He jabbed an admonitory finger toward her lips. "Mouth locked—remember? Maybe you don't care what a lot of strangers think, but what about your friends, everybody who knows you? And your uncle too, as far as that goes. How are you going to explain to them what happened to you up here last night? You can't! So they're going to think whatever they want to think, and it'll be all *wrong*."

A glance showed him his words were making an impression, and he hurried on. "And anyway, once you hit the street down there, you won't get farther than the first cop who sees you—and they'll haul you home like a silly runaway kid, and you'll be right back where you started from. No, you'll be worse off, because this whole thing—all these days and nights up here on this tower will turn out to be pointless—just a big fat *nothing*."

"No, Mike, no! To me never a big nothing! To me it—"

"To you, no—but to everyone else, yes!" He mashed his lips together and poked them with a ferocious finger. "Now will you just be *quiet*—and *listen?*"

The unexpected result of this ferocity was that she clapped both hands over her mouth, eyes widening enormously, and nodded with energetic penitence.

Michael hurried on, unable to pause for enjoyment of a masterful feeling. "Okay. What you need to do now is tear up that letter you were going to have somebody mail to your uncle and write another one. This time write it to Mam'selle Whoosis. She's the one that told you about the miracles, so she'll understand. Tell her you're safe and well and all that. Then tell her Notre Dame has done a miracle to you. Don't go into a lot of detail, just tell her it happened and that she's to tell your uncle you feel—you know—*different* about everything. You'll know how to say it. Then say you'll come home tomorrow—maybe at noon—and you hope your uncle will let you start fresh and. . . . Oh, heck—say what you want to. But that's the idea—to sort of prepare him, let him know something pretty big has happened to you, so then maybe he'll take a pretty good look at *him*self and—Now wait—wait!"

Dani still had her hands over her mouth but was beginning to look like a person who has blown up a very large balloon much too quickly. Michael wasn't quite ready yet for whatever explosion was building up. "Before you start yelling, let me tell you one more thing: What's going to happen, I'll bet anything, is that the newspapers will get hold of the letter. Well, not the letter, but the gist of it. They'll get it out of Mam'selle. So everybody will know that something important happened and that Notre Dame

did it! So it will all end with—well—with *dignity*. Now—
go ahead and yell."

But she didn't yell. She took her hands away from her
mouth and lowered them slowly and absentmindedly, regarding Michael with an expression of wonder. "Mike," she
said at last, "you are truly a—a—"

"Genius?" said Michael helpfully.

"Idiot!" corrected Dani. "You have forgotten that it is
today Saturday. This letter will go nowhere until Monday.
It will not reach Mam'selle until Tues—"

"It will reach Mam'selle this afternoon," Michael inter-
posed loftily. "Delivered by me, personally. Remember
what you told me, about how she goes to that café every
day, rain or shine, for her cup of chocolate? Well, today
she's going to have company!

"*Now.* What's French for 'genius'?"

19

Hands of the Law

As he started across the bridge from the Quai de la Tournelle on the Left Bank to the Ile St. Louis, Michael told himself disgustedly that there wasn't a reason in the world for his throat to be dry no matter how may times he swallowed. Nothing could possibly happen to him unless it was to get run over because he didn't watch where he was going.

Nor was there any reason to slap his right hip pocket every so often to make sure the letter was still there. How could it *not* be there when his jeans were so tight that nothing would fall out even if he walked on his hands? The mere thought of walking on his hands was appalling; what he needed now above all else was to be inconspicuous. The little man who wasn't there. Since there was nothing he could do to look any more inconspicuous than he already was, he concentrated on rehearsing yet again the movements just ahead of him.

They were so simple that even Charly could have performed them without straining his intellect. By continuing straight ahead for one block after leaving the bridge, he would reach the Rue St. Louis en l'Île, the only street that ran the length of the little island. There he would turn left and walk to the lower end of the island where the footbridge joined it to the Île de la Cité—the same footbridge he had crossed the night before in his flight from the policeman. At the intersection there he would find the Café Rouge et Blanc, where every day at three thirty Mlle. Henriette Duclos sat herself down to restore her strength and spirits with a steaming cup of chocolate.

On this particular day a nearby table would be occupied by an inconspicuous American boy with a letter in his pocket bearing her name on the envelope. The inconspicuous boy would be inconspicuously consuming a *glace vanille*. Finishing, he would get up, slip the letter (inconspicuously) within Mam'selle's reach, and stroll out the door, after which he would disappear in whichever direction was indicated by the inspiration of the moment. And that would be that. Nothing simpler. So there was nothing to be nervous about. Reaching the island end of the bridge, Michael swallowed, slapped his pocket, hunched himself deeper into a trenchcoat he wasn't wearing, and did his best to get back into the character of Magic Fingers Horner, who wouldn't have given a second thought to the possibility of something going wrong.

In this he wasn't very successful because he couldn't stop thinking about his parting—around an hour ago—from Dani. As he had slid the rather plump envelope into his pocket and prepared to go into his complicated departure routine, she had watched with a wistful look. "Always it is a time of sadness," she had said, "when something comes to an end." With a sweeping gesture she managed to embrace the parapet on which they stood, the gargoyles, the tower, the spire, the city spreading out below. "After tomorrow," she added, "all this will belong once more to the gargoyles. There will be no Mike here, and no Dani."

Michael had been aware of much the same feeling, but being both male and Anglo-Saxon, he couldn't admit it, and so he had grunted in a manner that sounded vaguely agreeable without actually agreeing to anything.

It had been the same way too, a little earlier, while Dani was busy writing the letter. It had taken her a long time to write it, and he had waited, lying on one of her blankets and watching little whipped-cream squirts of cloud drift over from the southeast to disappear above the summit of the tower. At one point she had interrupted this pleasant occupation with a large and plaintive sigh. "It is a very difficult task you have assigned," she said.

"Yup," he replied, "I'm a slave driver."

"Never before," she went on reflectively, "has it been my task to explain a miracle. And it is unfair that you should not help, for it is your miracle too."

"Yes, but it's *your* governess. Anyway I don't write French very well."

"Excuses. You are full of excuses. What will you say when you are an architect and you build a great building, and it falls down?"

"I'll say, 'Oops!' "

She laughed with delight. "Oops! I like oops." After that she was silent for so long, neither writing nor speaking, that Michael raised his head to look at her just as she turned and met his eye. "Your building will not fall down," she said with absolute assurance, returning from whatever far place she had been exploring. "You will be a fine architect. But first— First you will have to study very hard for a very long time, I think, at a university. It will cost a great deal of money."

Michael thought about the family Education Fund. "I'll be real brilliant," he said, "and win scholarships." He was enjoying the lazy clouds too much to be very serious about anything, and in a few moments Dani's pen resumed its faint scratching—at a faster pace, it seemed, than before.

Now, reaching the intersection with the Rue St. Louis, Michael brought himself back to the present moment and looked at his watch. Three fifteen. He was right on schedule. He turned to the left and immediately had the odd sensation that he had been spirited out of the middle of Paris and plunked down in a small French town. This main street was narrow, its traffic sparse and unhurried, the rush and roar of the great thoroughfares miraculously stilled. Two women stood chatting in front of a shop just ahead, each holding a string shopping bag. One stood on the curb, the other in the street, unconcerned about the traffic which at the moment consisted of an elderly bicyclist looking immensely dignified in his dark suit and beret. Both women spoke to him as he passed, and he replied, tipping his hat solemnly.

Farther up the street a half dozen or so small boys were playing a noisy but incomprehensible game involving numerous short sticks. It was as peaceful a scene as Michael had seen for a long time, and he felt some of his tension relax. The one really strange thing about the scene, had it occurred to him to think about it, was that there wasn't a policeman anywhere in sight.

What did occur to him, in an idle sort of way, was that most likely these people all knew Dani, at least by sight.

She lived at the lower end of the island in a luxurious apartment suite overlooking the Quai d'Orléans and the Seine and was the ward of one of the richest men on the island, yet Michael found it impossible to believe she would not be known to almost everyone. Dani simply wasn't the sort to go overlooked for long. Perhaps, he thought as he neared the women, they were talking about her now, speculating upon what fate might have befallen her. If only they knew that this boy strolling toward them, to whom they were paying no attention whatsoever, carried in his pocket a letter written scarcely an hour ago by that very girl. As he passed them, he strained his ears and linguistic abilities to the utmost but understood scarcely a word.

He continued on his way, pausing now and then to peer into a shopwindow for the sake of looking casual. Soon he reached an intersection, then another, and at last he saw the red-and-white striped awning of the Café Rouge et Blanc. In spite of himself, he swallowed hard to moisten his throat.

Aside from its name there was little to distinguish the café from hundreds scattered throughout Paris. On the sidewalk beneath the awning was the usual collection of little round tables, each with a metal chair or two. Only a few, Michael observed, were occupied. At one were two chattering women, one of whom held a toy poodle in her lap. Beside the chair of the other lay an enormous German shepherd. At another sat a trio of girls about Lucinda's age, chattering even harder than the women.

Michael went on inside because there, Dani had told him, was where Mam'selle always sat—at a table along the rear wall where she could chat with the proprietor's wife, who presided at the cash register.

Crossing the room to a table at the back, he felt ex-

tremely conspicuous. Two men were standing at the shiny
wooden bar with glasses of wine at hand. They glanced at
Michael. The man behind the bar, presumably the proprietor, who was shaped like a pigeon and wore a towel around
his middle, also glanced at Michael. The woman behind the
cash register wore a shapeless gray sweater and an afflicted
look. *She* glanced at Michael. A waiter in the customary
uniform of white jacket and tiny black snap-on bow tie
glanced too, and when Michael gained the refuge of a
table, he came slouching over, looking bored but available.

Michael swallowed just once more for good measure and
said, *"Une glace vanille, s'il vous plaît, m'sieu."*

"Une glace vanille!" the waiter echoed noisily as he
turned toward the man behind the bar.

After that, much to Michael's relief, nobody glanced at
him except the waiter when he brought the dish of ice
cream with the customary cardboard cookie sprouting
from its center. As his lips closed over the first spoonful
Michael felt an unexpected twinge of guilt. It didn't seem
right that he should be stuffing these delicious things into
himself while Dani still sat (or stood, or leaped, or danced)
up there on the cathedral tower with nothing but lukewarm pop to cheer her solitude.

Eating ice cream, however, was his "cover," as the spy
stories called it. Without ice cream he couldn't carry out
his mission. Conscience thus handily appeased, he ate with
the heartiness of virtue. In fact, he was about to spoon up
the last bite when he realized that there was still no sign of
Mlle. Duclos. With that last spoonful his cover would be
blown. There was only one thing to do, and he did it.
Managing to catch the eye of the waiter, he said politely,
"Encore une glace vanille, s'il vous plaît." There was just
no end to the sacrifices he was prepared to make for the

sake of the mission. Michael Horner, self-sacrificing secret agent.

The waiter had just set the second dish in front of him and removed the first when the woman at the cash register, who hadn't yet spoken a word, now suddenly spoke three in a voice that probably would have sliced through steel, like a laser beam. "Jacques, *Mam'selle vient!*" Mam'selle comes. Michael had no doubt that her Mam'selle and his were the same. If there had been doubt it would quickly have been dispelled by the way the man behind the bar snapped to the task of preparing a large cup of hot chocolate. Mam'selle, obviously, was a highly valued patron of the Rouge et Blanc. Michael, his throat going dry again in spite of all the ice cream, performed a complicated squirming maneuver to extract the letter from his pocket and slip it onto the chair under his leg where it would be quickly available. Then, secret-agentishly, he kept his eye on the door while seeming not to.

A few seconds later when the figure of Mlle. Duclos appeared in the doorway, Michael gaped with extremely *un*-secret-agentish lack of caution. Dani had not described her to him, and for reasons probably traceable to some book the word "governess" brought to his mind the picture of a large, bony, horsefaced female, middle-aged, wearing loose black garments and an expression of total disapproval. The reality was about as far from the picture as it could possibly be.

The Mlle. Duclos who entered with a cheery "Zhoomsdom," the customary telescoped version of "Bonjour, messieurs et mesdames," was younger than Michael's mother, almost as pretty, neither large nor the least bit bony, and with an expression which seemed to indicate that almost everything she saw was, if not pleasing, at least interesting. And she was dressed, Michael could tell, in a manner that would have inspired Lucinda to exclaim, to his annoyance, *"Très chic! Très à la mode!"* So much for horsefaced governesses.

The proprietress, who *was* horsefaced, seemed an unlikely person for this stylish young woman to have as a bosom friend, but they seemed to be on the best of terms and launched into a rattle of conversation as Mam'selle headed for the table next to Michael's. As she sat down, she tossed him a quick but disconcertingly thorough glance and then accepted with a word of thanks and a smile the steaming cup piled high with whipped cream which the proprietor bore to her table with an air of triumph. Michael began spooning ice cream into his mouth at a faster pace. The time had come to carry out his mission and get out of here.

At about this point his ear caught a tiny fragment of the cascading conversation. In a questioning tone the proprietress said something ending in *la petite.* He had small doubt who "the little one" was. From the corner of his eye he saw Mam'selle give her head a little shake. *"Rien de nouveau,"* she said. Nothing new.

The proprietress said something in a comforting tone, and Mam'selle changed the subject. Michael could tell by the slightly forced gaiety of her voice.

"So all right, what are you waiting for?" he asked himself, and responded by going into action in the deliberate manner the occasion called for. Fishing in his pocket, he got out four silver franc pieces and laid them on the table. This covered the price of the ice cream with a few centimes left over for a tip. Then he wiped his mouth with the tiny paper napkin in one hand and with the other slid the letter from under his leg and onto the edge of the table nearest to Mam'selle's, at the same time laying the napkin on top of it, carefully leaving the name on the envelope exposed—in Dani's handwriting.

The entire maneuver was most cleverly done, it seemed to him as he got to his feet and started toward the door. Mam'selle wouldn't notice the letter at once, or perhaps not at all, but if she didn't, the waiter would spot it the moment he came to get the money and clear the table. In either case, by the time it happened Michael would be out the door and across the Pont Louis Philippe to the Right Bank and the same metro station he had used in his escape the night before. Like all truly brilliant plans, it was very simple.

As he reached a point about midway between the table and the door, one of the wine-sipping customers at the bar performed an unhurried pivot on one foot and clamped a large, unyielding hand around Michael's upper arm. *"Bien-venue, mon brave!"* he said in a sardonic but not unkind tone. (Welcome, pal!) At the same moment the other man in two long strides crossed to the table, flipped the napkin away and picked up the letter. He glanced at the inscription on the envelope but his face gave no indication that it meant anything to him.

Though he felt paralyzed in the man's grip, Michael's mind, after an instant of gear slipping, was racing. What a moron he had been! With half a brain he could have figured out that the police would watch every move Mam'selle made on the chance that someone might approach her—someone with a message from the presumed kidnappers. Or she could be under suspicion herself. In either case he should have thought of it. But no, he had to go bulling around like a bird-brained buffalo. . . .

He pulled himself up short. There was no time to waste

in calling himself names. But what was there time *to* do? He was helpless. The cops had him. They had the letter, too, and apparently weren't even going to show it to Mam'selle. They would read it, they would know where Dani was, they would drag her ignominiously back to her uncle—and the whole miracle of Notre Dame might as well never have happened.

"Venez, donc!" rasped the voice of the detective who held Michael's arm, and he had no choice but to come along, heading for the door. But this was horrible! There must be *something* he could do before they dragged him off to a dungeon. There *had* to be! His darting eyes caught the stunned gaze of Mam'selle, who still sat at her table, apparently frozen with astonishment. In one of those lightning flashes that had been enlivening his exist-ence lately, it occurred to him that Mam'selle spoke excel-lent English, for it was she who taught Dani, and it was at least a possibility that the detectives spoke none at all. Twisting his neck to look at her even while being half dragged in the opposite direction, he shouted, "Miss Duclos! That letter—it's for you—from Dani! It's about the miracle of. . ." A large hand that stank of cheap cigarettes closed firmly and effectively over his mouth. At the same time the man's other arm slid around his waist just under the ribs, lifted him off the floor and hustled him out under the awning and around the corner to where a powerful-looking blue sedan stood at the curb.

Michael found himself shoved into the back seat, fol-lowed instantly by his captor, who shifted his grasp to Michael's wrist. The second detective—the one who had the letter—slid under the wheel and started the engine, all in a single movement.

The car was facing north, toward the Right Bank. Now it backed a few yards, made a smooth U-turn in the intersection and in a moment was gliding swiftly along the Quai d'Orléans toward the bridge over which Michael had crossed from the Left Bank scarcely thirty minutes before. As the U-turn was completed, with Michael's side of the car facing the Rouge et Blanc entrance, he caught sight of the elegant figure of Mam'selle as she burst out and came to an abrupt halt in the middle of the sidewalk. Her eyes were fixed, he felt sure, on him, even though there couldn't have been much of him to see. Then—and he felt a leaping inside him—she raised her right hand to her forehead and as the police car gathered speed made a deliberate and exaggerated sign of the cross.

She was telling him that she understood, even though he had got no further than the word "miracle." It must have been such a message, because there was nothing else it could have been. Furthermore, it was a message that only Michael could understand, and not the police, for they would have no way of knowing about Dani and Mam'selle and their talk of the miracles of Notre Dame. She was certainly smart, this governess, and amazingly quick. If he, Michael, had been even one-tenth as smart, he reflected bitterly, he wouldn't be riding in a dumb police car with a dumb detective and heading for— He didn't know for sure where he was heading, but he could bet it was the Prefecture of Police, that great buff-colored mass of masonry on the Île de la Cité facing Notre Dame across the Parvis.

He would have won the bet. The car crossed the Pont de la Tournelle to the Left Bank and turned right onto the quay, speeding westward past the next bridge and the next and the next. Then it swung right again, crossed the Pont St. Michel, right again on the Quai du Marche Neuf, and finally sharp left down a ramp and through a gate to a courtyard inside the monstrous building.

During the ride, which had taken scarcely five minutes,

not a word was spoken. Sooner or later, Michael decided, somebody was going to start asking him questions, and when they did, they were going to find out they'd got hold of the *dumbest* kid ever born in the U.S. of A.

The car halted on one side of the courtyard, and all three of its occupants got out—the detectives because they chose to, Michael because one of them had him by the wrist. This was a pretty stupid precaution, he thought, because even if he could get away, he couldn't run fifty feet without crashing into a policeman. The place was swarming with them.

Within another minute or two Michael had another excellent reason for not running away—he was completely lost. He had been led through so many doors, down so many corridors, up and down so many stairs, and around so many corners in this vast labyrinth of a place that he hardly knew left from right. But at last this peculiar safari came to an end in a medium-sized office in which there were two men, two desks, numerous filing cabinets and a huge map of Paris stuck full of colored pins. One of the men was in uniform, the other not. Both looked up as Michael and his escort entered. After the first glance the man in uniform ceased to exist and Michael found himself staring into the flint-hard eyes, as cold as outer space, of the man he had seen that first day up on the towers of Notre Dame.

While he stared into those eyes, the men who had brought him spoke rapidly in turn, their attitude showing they were reporting to a superior officer. Michael caught the word *Inspecteur*. One of them handed the inspector Dani's letter, and he dropped it to his desk without taking his eyes from Michael.

It seemed as if this silent scrutiny was destined to go on

forever, but at last the inspector motioned toward a straight-backed chair in front of his desk. *"Assieds-toi."*

Such was the force behind those cold eyes that Michael very nearly did sit down, recalling only at the last moment that he was now the dumb foreigner who couldn't understand a word of French. Behind him a voice said *"Il parle anglais."*

Again the inspector nodded toward the chair. "Please sit down," he said. After a moment Michael sat. No use pretending he couldn't understand English either. There was another unnerving pause, and then: "We have met. Can you tell me where?"

Michael shook his head, and the officer shrugged. "No matter. In time I shall remember." He leaned across the desk with a hand held out. "If you please—your identification."

Michael hesitated, but only for a moment, then got out his wallet and handed it over, convinced that if he didn't, they would simply take it. Thanks to Dad, it had all sorts of information in it, for use in case of emergency. The inspector looked through it without expression and made some notes on a pad. Tearing a sheet from the pad, he handed it to one of the detectives, who promptly left the room with his colleague. The inspector slit the letter open and slid from the envelope the wrinkled sheets of scratch paper covered with Dani's tightly written script. He spread these out on the desk and glanced up at Michael. "We will be more comfortable," he said, "if we do not talk until your father is present. I have sent for him." Leaving Michael to digest this bit of information, he turned his attention to the letter.

Unable to decide whether to be sorry or glad that Dad too was about to go for an unsolicited ride in a police car,

Michael gave up and concentrated on trying to detect some shadow of expression on the face of the inspector. With every moment that he watched, the tension mounted. At any moment now the inspector would leap to his feet yelling, "Aha—Notre Dame!" or something like that, and that would be the beginning of the end.

He should have known better. He should have known that not even the *new* Dani de la Tour could resist making the most of a dramatic situation. So he waited in vain for the explosion. Nothing happened except that at one point the inspector threw Michael an exceedingly penetrating look and came very close to throwing a question with it but restrained himself. He shuffled the pages of the letter together and began reading it all over again. Michael was in the middle of a sigh of relief when he jumped at the shrilling of a telephone—the one on the desk of the uniformed man whose existence he had all but forgotten.

The man answered with a sort of grunt, listened, then with a note of respect in his voice said, "*Un moment, m'sieu.*" Holding the phone away from his face, he turned to the inspector. "M'sieu Fernand de la Tour," he said.

Sprouting a third ear, Michael listened as the inspector answered, heard the crackle of a man's voice on the phone, and the inspector's replies, which he had no trouble understanding because they were simple, brief sentences. "Yes, m'sieu. That is true, No, not yet. At your convenience, m'sieu. Shall we send a car? Very well—enter from the Quai March Neuf. You will be met. Pardon? Ah—the good Mam'selle Duclos! She is here already! She waits outside my office, I am told—with extreme impatience. Yes. Very good."

Hanging up the phone, he sat in thought for a long moment, then opened a drawer and got out an enormous pipe with a curving stem. He loaded it, set it afire with all the meticulous attention Michael remembered from Dad's pipe-smoking days, and peered out from the resulting blue-gray cloud. Then an incredible thing happened. Like a crack slowly opening in a glacier, a knife-thin rift in a mass of cloud, a smile appeared on the craggy face, followed at a glacial pace by a grin that exposed a set of strong, square, yellowish teeth.

"In a very few minutes, my young friend," said the inspector, "you are going to find yourself the center of a great deal of attention."

Even if there had been anything to say, Michael couldn't possibly have said it. That grin had stricken him dumb.

The inspector blew another streamer of smoke. "But until the storm breaks over you, I suggest that you remain in that uncomfortable chair and meditate upon the crimes with which it may soon become my duty to accuse you."

"C-crimes?" Michael said, finding a small, unreliable fragment of his voice.

"But of course!" The inspector began ticking them off on a handful of big fingers. "One: withholding information from the police. That is a very serious offense. Two: giving assistance and encouragement to a fugitive. Three—"

"But, sir, I—"

"Three: refusal to cooperate in a police investigation. Four—"

"I didn't refuse! I only—"

The inspector raised his voice. "Four: by devious and no doubt unlawful means winning the affection of a young female citizen of the Republic of France. And *that*, my friend, is a crime akin to treason! So meditate, I beg of you, and before it is too late—repent!" With that he picked up some papers from his desk and immersed himself in a study of them.

Michael, whose ears, face, and finally his whole head

had turned hot as flame, proceeded to meditate, if that was what it could be called, about what in the world the fiendish Dani could have said about him in the letter. When he had got nowhere with that and given up trying— and his ears had cooled off—there was time left to meditate about how altogether incredible it was that a Parisian detective inspector who looked quite capable of carving a criminal into small pieces and eating them for lunch should actually be a sort of kindly ogre. A detective inspector, furthermore, who obviously had been investing days of his time and energy in directing the search for a missing young female citizen of the Republic of France who now turned out to be missing of her own free will and in no danger at all. And yet he didn't appear to be even mildly angry about it.

A few minutes later Michael's father was escorted politely into the office by a uniformed policeman. He had time for only one bewildered look at Michael before the inspector claimed his attention. "Ah, m'sieu—I am Inspector Delaude. You must accept my apologies for taking you away from your work. Because you and your family are guests of my country, it seemed proper that you should be present during our interrogation of your son."

Michael saw his father's Adam's apple do something gymnastic before he replied. "That's very kind of you Inspector. What has he—what has he done?"

The inspector indicated a second chair that looked just as uncomfortable as Michael's. "Please be seated, *M'sieu le Professeur*. It will take him a considerable time to tell you."

M'sieu le Professeur looked uncertainly from the inspector to Michael and back again. "For *him* to tell me?"

The inspector nodded. "A few minutes ago I outlined to

him the charges I may see fit to bring against him. Michael, will you repeat to your father those charges?"

Michael stared at him in consternation and for a moment thought he was about to gain a reprieve because the inspector suddenly barked, "One moment!" and turned to his subordinate. "Chavannes, please go inform Mlle. Duclos that I will see her now. Quickly. And bring another chair."

Quickly was scarcely the word for it. Almost as soon as the door had closed behind the officer, Michael heard the rapid click of feminine heels in the corridor, followed by the neat, stylish figure of the governess, who lost no time at all in loosing a whole flight of verbal arrows at the inspector—in French. Michael caught enough of it to know that she was indignantly demanding to know what he knew about Dani and what right the police had to snatch from her very hands a letter addressed to her.

Favoring her with one of his sub-zero stares, the inspector said, "This interview, Mam'selle, is being conducted in the English language. Do you speak it?"

Without deigning to answer the question, she began to repeat her demand in English. But the inspector halted her with a gesture. "For the present," he said, "you will listen. You will be given an opportunity to speak later. At the moment this young man is about to repeat to his father the offenses with which he may be charged. Michael, you may commence."

In desperation Michael glanced from one to another. Mam'selle looked sympathetic but helpless. Dad looked willing but baffled. The inspector looked like a chunk of granite. "Well," Michael began, "the inspector said—" He paused, observing a tendency in his voice to get all gummy, like brand X motor oil. Clearing his throat, he started over.

"The inspector said I was guilty of withholding information from the police and—uh—assisting and encouraging a fugitive." He did an imitation of somebody trying hard to remember.

"And the third?" growled the inspector, who apparently lacked sympathy for feeble memories.

"The third was—uh—refusing to cooperate in a police investigation!" Michael produced this with an unconvincing air of triumphant finality.

Dad, at any rate, accepted this innocent little dodge at face value. "Well, Mike," he said, "that's a pretty serious—"

"Your pardon, sir," interrupted the inspector. Great interrupters, police inspectors. "There is one more."

"There—there is?" bleated Michael, wishing he were six years old and dimpled. "I guess I can't remember that one."

The inspector leaned back in his chair and crossed his fingers behind his head. "We shall wait," he said with an air of infinite patience, "until your memory returns."

If he was lucky, Michael thought, he might die just standing there. Thud. He waited hopefully but nothing happened. Just not his lucky day. Maybe he could say it in a kind of fast mumble—but the inspector would never let him get away with it. Nothing to do but bite the bullet. "The fourth one," he said, severely eyeing his father's necktie, "was about winning the—um—affections of a young French—um—female citizen."

Hot as fire one more, and skewered on three sharp sets of eyes, Michael felt like a shish kebab. It was one of those moments that could end only in one way: a babble of voices.

"A young French—good heavens, Mike!" exclaimed Dad.

"I demand to know—" began Mam'selle.

"Sir," said Chavannes, whose phone had just rung, "M'sieu de la Tour has arrived."

"He is to come in," said the inspector.

If I can't drop dead, said Michael to himself, maybe I could just go into a coma.

20

Unfinished
Miracle

In a good many ways the next thirty minutes or so of
Michael's life was like the time he fell out of a tree at the
age of eight and broke his arm: pretty awful while it was
going on, but he wouldn't have missed it.

To begin with, his first glimpse of Fernand de la Tour
was something of a shock. In a vague way he had expected
something like a cartoonist's conception of an industrialist: jowls, paunch, big cigar. The man who strode quickly
through the door as Chavannes opened it and stood re-
spectfully aside was of medium height and slight build,
with a full head of hair graying at the sides, a clean-shaven
face deeply tanned, and clothes that even Michael could
recognize as tastefully elegant. His movements were quick,
athletic, and gave the impression of energy and force.

The real shocker was his eyes. Below heavy wedges of brow they were dark, searching, and restlessly active. They were so much like Dani's eyes—except, of course, for not being pretty—that the effect was slightly unnerving. Right now those eyes, in spite of the tanned skin, were deeply circled, as though Fernand de la Tour hadn't been sleeping well lately.

They moved quickly, scanning each face in turn, and lingering longest on Michael's, which apparently he found the most interesting. Then the inspector spoke, inviting him to sit down (it was more like a command), explaining why English was being spoken, and performing the introductions. Except for his forbidding appearance, Michael thought, he could have been the host of one of those television talk shows on which guests are encouraged to disagree with one another. They sat in a semicircle in front of the inspector's desk so that everybody could look at him (and be looked at) and at one another as well. As the only nonadult on the premises, Michael felt as outnumbered as General Custer's cavalry at the Little Bighorn.

"*Alors!*" began the inspector, momentarily forgetting himself. "Very well! I will begin at the beginning." He glanced at his watch. "About one hour ago this young man, Michael Horner, was apprehended as he attempted to deliver to Mlle. Duclos a letter written to her by Danielle de la Tour, who has been the object of a police search for five days. This letter is now in my possession. I have read it. And unless it proves to be an almost impossibly elaborate forgery, the young lady is safe and well and expects soon to return to her home—*your* home, of course, M'sieu de la Tour."

Michael sneaked a quick look at Uncle Fernand, who looked tense and strained, as if holding himself under rigid control.

The inspector turned to Mam'selle. Leaning across his desk, he handed her the envelope. "Can you identify the handwriting?"

She glanced at it and said tartly, "I can. But it would be better if I were to see the letter itself."

"In good time," said the inspector affably. It has been read by no one but myself. Unless"— he paused, like a pitcher eyeing the runner at first base, then whirled and fired his knuckleball straight at Michael's head —"unless *you* have read it. Tell me, Michael—*did* you read this letter?"

Michael felt his body recoil, as if from a threat of harm. The kindly ogre had turned himself into a cobra. "N-no, sir!" he blurted. "I didn't!"

"Perhaps you did not *need* to read it because this letter was your idea. Perhaps you told Danielle de la Tour what to write in this letter. Is that true?"

"Well, now, hold everything, Inspector. You have no reason to—"

Michael felt a warm wave of gratitude as he glanced at his father. Good old Dad—the more disturbed he was, the slower and drawlier he talked—but Michael was getting practically superstitious about this Supercop. If you didn't tell him the whole truth and nothing but, he'd drag it out of you. "I didn't tell her *what* to write," he said, interrupting Good Old Dad, "but writing anything at all was my idea."

"I see," said the inspector, managing to imply that what he saw reflected scant credit on Michael. "Can you tell us *why* you desired this letter to be written?"

"No, sir, I can't."

"Can't—or won't?"

Michael shrugged, beginning to feel stubborn. "If she—if the letter doesn't explain it, *I* can't."

"Mam'selle!" The inspector switched to a new victim. "It was reported to me that as this boy was being taken into custody, he called to you, saying something about a miracle. Is that correct?"

She nodded.

"And did that word hold some particular significance for you?"

Mam'selle shrugged the eloquent Gallic shrug that can mean yes, no, maybe, I don't know, or none of your business.

"Enough significance," pursued the inspector, "that it inspired you to rush out on the street and make the sign of the cross?"

Mam'selle elevated her chin. "For how long," she inquired, "have a citizen's devotions been of concern to the police?"

The inspector inclined his head in a courtly manner. "Thank you, Mam'selle. You have answered my question. And now—"

"I ask your pardon, Inspector," put in Uncle Fernand crisply, "but does it truly serve your purpose to—ah—browbeat a young woman and a mere boy?"

Michael was deciding he didn't care much for that "mere" when he saw the inspector turn his head with great deliberation to favor the younger man with an arctic look. "When my duty requires it, m'sieu," he said, "I also browbeat men of wealth and importance."

"Well now, I don't know—" This was Dad, who had stretched his long legs out and hooked his toes under the edge of the inspector's desk, so that he could tip his chair back—a sure sign that he was beginning to enjoy himself— and such was the power of suggestion that Michael actually felt that just about any minute now he might start enjoying himself too. "Doesn't seem to me," continued Dad, "that anybody's brow has been beaten much yet. So if we'll all just answer the questions we're asked, the inspector can wrap this thing up and we can all go home."

"Thank you, Professor Horner," the inspector said. "Do I take it that you are volunteering?"

Dad smiled. "I'm willing, but I don't know much."

"Very well. Do you include, among the things you *do* know, the whereabouts of Danielle de la Tour?"

Dad shook his head. "No, I don't know where she is."

"But you can guess?"

Dad's hesitation was almost imperceptible. "Yes."

"But you do not choose to disclose what you guess?"

"I'm afraid not."

"Because of loyalty to your son?"

"Something like that."

The inspector nodded. "Very commendable." Michael couldn't tell whether he meant to be approving or sarcastic. "And now, Mam'selle, we return to your—er—devotional activities." He picked up Dani's letter. "In this there is another appearance of the word 'miracle.' The writer refers to *le miracle de la Vierge* — the miracle of the Virgin. Does that phrase convey to you—Ah, I see that it does."

Michael had been so lost in admiration that he missed Mam'selle's muffled exclamation, which told the inspector what he wanted to know. The admiration was for Dani's cleverness. The Virgin, Our Lady, and Notre Dame were all one and the same, of course, except to somebody who understood that the cathedral was meant, rather than Her for whom it was named. It was, in effect, a sort of private code.

The inspector was forging on with his interrogation, and

Michael had a feeling he had better pay attention and stay on his toes. "And what, Mam'selle, does 'the miracle of the Virgin' convey to you with respect to the whereabouts of Danielle de la Tour?"

Michael found himself holding his breath. Slanting his eyes around at the governess, he found her doing the same toward her employer. Then she turned back to the inspector and said in a tone both apologetic and defiant. "It tells me—where Danielle is to be found."

"*Amour de Dieu*, mam'selle!" Uncle Fernand half rose from his chair, but the inspector raised a peremptory hand. "*Soyez tranquil!* Be calm, if you please. And if *you* please, Mam'selle Duclos, disclose to us now the location of this place."

Again there was silence. Mam'selle, it seemed to Michael, carefully avoided Uncle Fernand's eyes, encountering instead those of Dad. He smiled encouragingly at first and then, to Michael's shocked but delighted astonishment, slowly and solemnly winked, whereupon she turned to the inspector once more. "I regret," she said, "but I cannot tell you this. To do so would betray a confidential matter, between Danielle and me."

"Ah!" said the inspector dryly. "Another demonstration of loyalty. This room, it overflows with loyalty! And now—"

"Mam'selle!" This time Uncle Fernand did get to his feet. "If you know where Dani is, you *must* tell. She must come home—she belongs with me—under my roof! And you, Professor Horner, it is an unkind thing you do! You cannot know—"

"*Please, m'sieu!*" The inspector spoke commandingly. "We have arrived now at a question which has long been in my mind. If you will please to be seated again, perhaps we shall soon come to the end of this affair."

After a pause Uncle Fernand sat down reluctantly and, placing a hand over his eyes, massaged them. It was a weary sort of gesture, and Michael felt a stab of sympathy, perhaps a little guilt. Fernand de la Tour was no longer just a name or a thing in a newspaper called a well-known industrialist. He was a troubled and unhappy man.

"The question," began Inspector Delaude, only to be interrupted by the telephone. Chavannes answered, listened, and turned to the inspector. *"Les journalistes!"* he hissed in a sort of stage whisper.

"Sacré!" swore the inspector. A very mild oath, but his tone made it savage. He picked up his own phone and ripped out an order in the same tone—probably, Michael thought, to have the journalists hung by their thumbs until further notice.

He then addressed himself once more to Uncle Fernand as if no interruption had occurred. "The question that has troubled me, m'sieu, is this: Why does a child such as your neice choose to run away from her home?"

Uncle Fernand's slim figure stiffened as he met the inspector's eyes. "If you think, *m'sieu l'inspecteur*, that I have not thought of this, again and again, then you are no judge of men."

"And I find only one answer," the inspector went on as if he were talking to himself, as if the other man had said nothing at all. "The child runs away because in the home she is unhappy. Wait! There is no need to explain that you have given the child everything, spared no expense. All the world knows you are a man of wealth, and of honor, and that you have offered a large reward for her safe return. One moment, m'sieu. Will you permit me to ask one question? It is not asked idly, I assure you."

After a prolonged hesitation Fernand de la Tour nodded curtly. "Thank you," the inspector said. "My question is this: *Why* do you offer this large sum? *Why* do you so greatly desire the return of the little Danielle?"

Michael watched with fascination as the younger man digested this challenge. Obviously not accustomed to answering the questions of policemen or anyone else, he appeared to be trying to remain as expressionless as the inspector but not succeeding very well. Now he snapped, "The answer to that should be obvious."

"Perhaps it should, m'sieu, but the obvious answer is not always the true one."

"Would the inspector care to explain?"

It looked to Michael as if the two pairs of eyes were locked together, that the two of them had forgotten there was anyone else present.

"There is the possibility," said the inspector, "that your concern is less with your niece than it is with your reputation—your *image* as they call it these days."

"My image be damned!" Uncle Fernand suddenly was on his feet, obviously controlling his anger with great difficulty. "I want my niece back for reasons that are no concern of yours, and if you cannot restore her to me, I will go over your head and find a policeman who can!"

"A policeman, m'sieu, who will kiss your foot?" The inspector's voice was as coldly calculating as his eyes. "A policeman who will not ask of you embarrassing questions? A policeman who will not require you to be honest with yourself?"

Now, Michael thought. Now comes the explosion!

Seconds went by as he held his breath, footsteps and voices crescendoed and receded in the corridor outside, more seconds passed—and nothing happened. No explosion.

The sound Michael made as he let out his breath and

took a new one was overlaid by the screech of the inspector's chair as he slid it back and stood up, picking up the letter from his desk. He looked down at it, breaking at last the locked-in gaze the two men had been holding. "In this letter, m'sieu," he said, "is much to be learned about honesty with one's self. I think the time now has come for you to learn of the miracle of Notre Dame."

Turning unexpectedly he asked, "Mam'selle—do you read well aloud?"

She nodded uncertainly, and he went on. "Good. The letter is for you, but perhaps you will be good enough to read it to M'sieu de la Tour. I will send you to a room where you may be private."

Again he met the eyes of Fernand de la Tour, who returned the gaze levelly and at last shook his head in a bemused, unbelieving way, and reverted to his own language. *"Etes-vous sorcier, M'sieu?"*

Under all pressures of the moment Michael's translating apparatus failed to function until the door had closed behind the silent pair, escorted by Chavannes. Then it did a playback. "Are you a sorcerer?" Uncle Fernand had asked.

Now he turned to find the sorcerer-policeman watching him with an all but imperceptible glint of amusement in his eyes and remembered his words of a few moments before: "The time now has come for you to learn of the miracle of Notre Dame." Not "La Vierge," or "Our Lady," but "Notre Dame." So he must know.

His next words dispelled all doubt. "So, young Michael, you have accomplished your mission—more effectively, perhaps, than you could have hoped."

"You remembered," Michael said. "Where you first saw me, I mean."

The inspector shrugged—a small shrug for one so large. "I am trained to remember such things." He sat down behind the desk slowly, and it occurred to Michael that he might be older than he looked. "And now," he went on, "it will no longer be necessary, I think, for your prettiest gargoyle to spend another night away from home."

"How did you— Oh." Michael's brain was acting like Charly's again. The letter, of course, No telling what was in it.

"She wrote," said the inspector solemnly, "that it is better to be the prettiest gargoyle than the queen of France."

There was a pause during which Michael wished he could turn into an inanimate object. Dad came to the rescue. "Not much of a choice—since there hasn't been a French queen since 1789."

"Since 1870, m'sieu. Have you forgotten the Empress Eugénie?"

"Empresses don't count, Inspector"—Dad leaned forward, his tone changing—"there's a lot I don't understand yet about all this. But one thing I know—I've been privileged to watch a master at work. A master of human relationships."

"No, no. What you have been watching, *M'sieu le Professeur*, is an old *flic*—an old cop—who is going soft in the head." The inspector began making meaningless marks on a note pad. "No, that is not true, not altogether." For a moment he watched himself doodle, then with the air of one who has reached a decision, "Messieurs. . . Messieurs, there are times when it is easier to speak to strangers in a foreign tongue than to one's own people—of things that are near to the heart. You, *M'sieu le Professeur*, have heard now about the miracle of Notre Dame. You do not yet know what it means—but you may accept my word that you are part of it. Your son here is at the center of it—he and the little Danielle—but it embraces others, as in time you will see. And one of them is the old cop. I will explain. Soon it will be forty years since I became a policeman. I—" His telephone shrilled an interruption, and he glared at it with annoyance before scooping it up—an annoyance shared by Michael. No telling what revelations might be forthcoming from this unpredictable policeman.

"Delaude *ici!*" the inspector snapped into the offending instrument. As it turned out, these were the only words comprehensible to Michael in all the crackling conversation that followed, though he somehow got the idea that it had to do with a robbery. When it was over, the inspector replaced the receiver on its cradle and stared at it a moment with a wry expression. "An invention of the devil, the telephone," he remarked. "But it has many uses. For example, it has today prevented a sentimental old cop from"—he frowned, groping for words—"you Americans have one of your lively expressions—something about weeping—crying—"

"Crying into your beer?" Dad suggested with a smile.

"Exactly!" The inspector sounded triumphant. "The old cop was about to cry into his beer. Now I will not do so. I will say only that a bit of your miracle has—how do you say? —rubbed off. It has rubbed off on me, and given to me some added strength which I could not find—here." A big fist thumped the center of the inspector's chest.

Michael stared at the fist, and the crag of a face above it. They seemed to hold all the strength that any man had need of.

But the inspector was jerking open a drawer, from which he extracted a sealed envelope. This he regarded sardonically for a moment before tearing it in two and dropping the halves into his wastebasket. Then he looked across the desk at father and son, whose expressions, Michael thought later, must have been comically and identically bewildered, because he suddenly bared his teeth in a genuine, though slightly wolfish grin. "That, messieurs," he explained, "was my resignation, my application for early retirement." To Michael he added, "Because of you, *mon enfant*, and your Danielle, and your miracle, the city of Paris must endure me for another three years."

Michael had time only to wonder in an awed sort of way about whatever in the world Dani could have said in that letter to produce all these astonishing results when the inspector reared to his feet and footsteps sounded in the corridor. A voice spoke in an undertone and the door opened, the blue-clad arm of Chavannes holding it.

The first to enter was Mam'selle, who gave the impression of a woman who has just taken a deep breath and elevated her chin for the purpose of holding onto the control of her emotions. Michael saw her eyes, which were luminous, pass over the inspector as if he were part of the furniture and fasten on his own. Instantly they filled with tears, and she started toward him.

She was going to kiss him; all the signs pointed to it. With a mother, a sister, three aunts, and two grandmothers, he couldn't be wrong about a thing like that. He wasn't. . . and she did. . . and it wasn't bad at all, really. She had a very pleasant scent; she planted a solid kiss on his cheekbone, murmured some French at him, and tactfully turned away.

Fernand de la Tour glanced first at Michael, an unreadable expression in his eyes. Then he reached across the desk and shook hands with the inspector in a stiff, formal manner. "Your words were not wasted, Inspector," he said. "I shall always be in your debt."

The inspector growled something in reply, but Uncle Fernand was already turning toward Michael with hand outstretched, and for the first time Michael saw him smile. This in itself was rather unnerving, for there, was, eerily, something of Dani in the smile. Then his hand was firmly grasped and shaken with a cordiality which Michael knew he couldn't possibly deserve.

"And to you, my young friend, I owe much for which I cannot thank you."

Michael could do nothing but stare up at him and try not to look too much like Charly. Mercifully, Uncle Fernand went on. "For one thing, my niece has informed me, by means of this letter to Mam'selle Duclos, that you are responsible for her decision to return home and to accompany me willingly to America."

Like most people, Michael wasn't above accepting a little credit where credit wasn't due—but this was too much. "N-no sir!" he burst out, stumbling a little because it was news even to him that Dani had decided to go to America, willingly or otherwise. "*I* didn't make her decide anything. It was the music, and the—"

"The miracle!" put in Mam'selle obligingly and with great firmness.

"That's right," Michael said gratefully. "I only—"

"She wrote," Uncle Fernand went on, "that it was you who insisted she undertake the letter—for the sake of the *dignity* of us all. Is that not so?"

"Well," Michael said uncomfortably, remembering that he had indeed spoken of dignity, "I just thought it would be—well—*neater* all around to do it that way."

Uncle Fernand nodded soberly. "And so it has come about—very neatly indeed. Thanks to you and to the inspector."

"Well, gosh," Michael began in a burst of honesty, "I don't get any credit—I loused it up, really—because I didn't *plan* to get caught by the police."

"But you did get caught—and that is of the first importance, because it was the inspector who has set me straight about Fernand de la Tour."

The last was directed not to Michael but to the inspector, who smiled his faint and frosty smile. "Perhaps it would surprise you to know, m'sieu, that I too have been set straight by these events—by this miracle."

"After this day," said Uncle Fernand with an answering smile, "nothing will surprise me." He turned to Michael's father. "And now, sir, I have a proposal for which I must ask your permission?"

Looking just as startled as Michael felt, Dad said, "*My* permission?"

The other nodded. "It is proper that I consult you. But let me explain." He looked around, pulled his chair closer to Dad's and sat down, leaning toward him in a manner that seemed effectively to exclude everyone else in the room.

"For some years I have maintained a fund to help with the education of young men who show exceptional promise. Thus far these young men have been French. But now that my company plans to open a branch in America—in San Francisco—it seems appropriate that this assistance should go also to American boys. I propose that your son be the first of these."

Dad stared from Uncle Fernand to Michael and back again. "But why Michael? You said 'exceptional promise.' You don't know whether Michael shows any promise at all. And to be quite honest—neither do I!"

Uncle Fernand's smile broadened. Now he was the one

who was beginning to enjoy himself. "What you and I think, m'sieu, is beside the point. Mam'selle!"

"*Oui*, M'sieu?"

"Read, if you please, the postscript—for the enlightenment of *M'sieu le Professeur*."

Nodding happily, the governess shuffled through the pages of the letter and began to read, translating as she went:

"This postscript, my dear uncle, is to you. Until this moment I have been humble and repentant and very, very saintly—and I shall be so again, as soon as I have asked this one very small favor.

"I cannot prove it, but nevertheless I *know* that someday Michael will be a fine architect and create many beautiful things. But he will need the most expensive of educations—and his father's suits are all made with poverty pockets. He himself has said so. So please may I suggest that you add to your list of deserving scholars the name of Michael Horner. If you do so, he will be *sure* to build these beautiful buildings and the world will be forever grateful to you. And so too will your obedient, humble, repentant, and saintly—Dani.

"Post-postscript: The cost, I think, will be much less than fifty thousand francs, which he could have claimed from you at any time had he not been true to his Prettiest Gargoyle."

Folding up the letter, Mam'selle gave Michael a brilliant smile, to which the prominent industrialist added a smile of his own. Dad, on the other hand, shook his head, frowning a little. "What you propose," he said, "would be to my benefit as much as to Mike's—and whatever he may or may not have done to deserve it *I've* certainly done nothing, so—"

"On the contrary," Uncle Fernand interrupted emphatically, "you have done a great deal! You were my 'friend at court,' so to speak. Besides, m'sieu, thanks to the miracle of Notre Dame I too am inspired to be saintly, humble, and repentant—and Danielle's request now presents me with the rare opportunity to be all of these fine things at a—how do you say in America—a *cut rate*. Surely, m'sieu, would not deny to me so great an opportunity!"

Dad could only grin and shrug. "Play it your way, M'sieu de la Tour. Darned if I'm going to be the only little skunk at the party."

Now the inspector got into the act. "That role, M'sieule Professeur," he said, "is reserved for the police. Michael!"

"S-sir!" Michael jumped visibly.

"I have decided I will make no charges against you for your crimes—on one condition."

"Yes, sir?" Even though he knew the inspector's severity was a put-on, he couldn't keep his voice altogether steady. Everything—the setting, the company, the all but incredible things that were happening to everyone and particularly to Michael Horner—combined to give him the feeling that any moment now the trapdoor in the Fun House floor would drop and send him zipping down the chute.

"You will climb once more the towers of Notre Dame. You will burden yourself with the belongings of Mam'selle Danielle de la Tour. You will then descend with her to the earth we ordinary mortals tread and escort her to her home."

"But, sir, Inspector!" Michael had been squirming inwardly, torn between the need to speak and a reticence about interrupting. "Sir, it's almost six o'clock—and the tower's locked up at five!"

There was a silence that managed to sound full of

amusement; then Dad spoke. "Mike, I rather imagine that if the inspector asks *real* politely, they'll open it up again."

While Michael grinned sheepishly for lack of a more intelligent reaction, the inspector said, "I will send two *extremely* polite policemen with you—in an unmarked car."

Michael said nothing to this announcement, though he wondered mightily why he needed a car to travel the hundred yards or so from the Prefecture to the cathedral. Apparently, though, the others were looking baffled too, and the inspector explained. "The press. They swarm. They have learned we are questioning an American boy who has a connection with Danielle de la Tour. Best you go, Michael, before the swarm grows thicker. Off you go now—follow M'sieu Chavannes. And *au revoir!* We shall meet again, I promise you!"

21

Back to

Earth

"How," asked Dani gravely, "does one say good-bye to a gargoyle?"

She had just edged her way between the iron grille and the gargoyle with the prominent elbows on the inner side of the south tower and was still standing on the balustrade with one hand resting on the creature's head. She was wearing the tanager-colored sweater again, and the blue stretch pants, and the declining sun which had now passed a little north of west reached into this corner and embraced the colors warmly.

Michael, who had preceded her, stood looking up from the walkway below, her pack strapped to his back with Old Longview sticking out the top, and a bundle at his feet. The sun made glinty highlights on her short black hair, which she had insisted on combing carefully while he held her tiny mirror. For a moment of stillness her small, eager profile was sharply outlined against the deep blue of the sky to the east, and Michael felt a stab of an old familiar haunting emotion. Because it was so far removed from what he was seeing now, it took him a long moment to recognize it.

It was the feeling that gripped him several times each autumn at home when the courageous, urgent, mournful cries of a flight of wild geese impelled him outside in any weather to watch the shallow, shifting V of a score or more pairs of steadily beating wings, jet black against the low gray skies as they followed their ancient pathway through the air. To him the sight, no matter how often he saw it, was always mournful and troubling and uplifting and beautiful beyond understanding. It made him want at the same time to cry tears and to yell with joy, and as a result, he merely stood in silent awe, feeling the beat of the wings in his blood and bones.

It was like that now. He could only stand, earthbound and stodgy, and look up at this wing-footed creature of air and light who was followed around by miracles.

She must have felt this look of his, for she turned quickly and smiled. "How *does* one, Michael—how does one say good-bye to a gargoyle?"

He looked down quickly, fearful that all those high-flown things might show in his eyes. "You don't *need* to," he said, sounding grumpy when he meant only to sound matter-of-fact, "because you can come up here any time you want to."

She gave him her serious, considering look, then shook her head decisively. "It will not be the same." Jumping lightly down beside him, she added, "When I come again—

if I come again—I will be only a visitor. I will be a *guest* of the gargoyles, but no longer will I be one of them. Never again *can* I be one of them."

He nodded, feeling quite sure that he understood. "I know what you mean—and you *can't* say good-bye. You can't *ever* say good-bye, and it's silly to try." How, he asked himself, could he be so sure that what he said was so? But he *was* sure. "All you can do is turn around and go. So come on, let's do it."

He squatted down awkwardly, encumbered as he was, and picked up the bundle, which consisted of books and other things wrapped in the jacket he had lent her, the sleeves knotted around it. "Here." She slipped one arm underneath the knot and held the bundle awkwardly against her hip and he led the way to the front of the tower, jogging around the corner where another pair of monsters stood guard. Now they could look down to the busy street, the Parvis, the vast bulk of the Prefecture and the Palace of Justice beyond, the Seine to the left, and the roofs of Paris everywhere.

In the middle of the open space between the towers Dani halted him with a touch on the arm. Without looking at him, she set the bundle down and leaned her arms on the parapet, looking outward. After a moment he leaned too, waiting. Waiting for what? He didn't know—but he knew it was important. At last she said, "It is very strange, but I think that I do not wish to go back—to the earth. Up here I have been"—she fluttered her hands, seeking words—"not happy, not contented, but—oh, how do you say it?—*at peace.* I have been at peace. It is silly, I know, but at this moment I feel that I could stay here forever, as long as"—half turning, she looked squarely at him—"as long as I could have Mike to—to—"

Quicksand seemed to be shifting beneath Michael's feet,

and he forced a shaky sort of grin. "I know—to bring you peanut butter and jelly sandwiches."

Now she turned all the way, facing him with her back against the parapet, and he was appalled to see that her eyes had welled with tears, and he was drowning in them. There was only one way to save himself, and he took it.

In Michael's experience up to that moment kissing had been something done to a person by his female relatives. A sort of minor inconvenience that didn't do him any harm and seemed to make them feel good. But now, in a matter of a second or two he learned he had been living in the deepest abyss of ignorance and darkness. Suddenly he was Copernicus and Galileo and Newton and Einstein discovering the secrets of the universe, and Notre Dame de Paris hiked up her skirts and did a ponderous pirouette before settling back on her ancient underpinnings, and Michael Horner, dizzy in the head, backed off, babbling, "and sody-pop, and cans of glurp, and books to read, and batteries for your radio, and—and for gosh sakes, I don't see anything to *cry* about!"

For a long time, it seemed, she looked at him, and at last her lips turned up, and she smiled "I cry," she said, "because when I go down from here, I will get no more peanut butter and jelly sandwiches."

"Wait till you come to Oregon," he told her, relieved that she was willing to let this serious moment passs in a joking way. "You can have them three times a day. Hey, I know—we'll go skiing and take a whole box full of—"

She interrupted him with a hand on his arm, looking worried. "My uncle—did he say he would take me to Oregon—once we have gone to San Francisco, I mean?"

"Well, no, he didn't *say* so, but I'll bet he will." Grinning, he added, "How can he refuse you anything—with

you so humble and reformed and dutiful and saintly and—
and all that?" He shrugged the pack to a slightly more
comfortable spot on his back. "Anyway, right now I've got
orders from the inspector to take you home." He led the
way along the parapet and the zigzagging balcony to the
far corner of the north tower, where the "Taking Down to
Forbid" sign stood. In spite of it this was the way they
would descend, the police having opened only this stairway, not the one in the south tower ordinarily used for
descent.

Here, in the shadow of Charly and his big bird of a
friend, they paused by common, unspoken consent for a
lingering look around. While Dani peered down toward the
earth of ordinary mortals Michael lifted his eyes, and
there, in engagingly monstrous silhouette, loomed the profile of Charly. Under his breath, far too softly to be heard
by anyone, Michael said, "Thanks, Charly—thanks for the
introduction."

Charly—right on the job—strictly business—no distrac-
tions—said nothing, but suddenly Dani did. "Mike! All
those people—look!"

Michael peered down to where she pointed. On the
sidewalk at the foot of the buttress he saw a small, milling
knot of people, mostly men. Now and then the top of
one's head would turn into a face as he looked upward.
"Hey!" he exclaimed, suddenly remembering. "It's the
newspapermen, Dani—*les journalistes!* The inspector said
they were swarming—and I guess that's the swarm."

Instead of a swarm, he thought, they were more like a
congregation of cats at a mousehole—the mousehole being
the only exit from this tower. He didn't say so, though, for
Dani looked aghast enough already. "Journalists! They
will have cameras! Mike, what can we do?"

"Go down," he said. "Nothing else we *can* do. Go down and let them take our picture!"

With a mother and a sister, not to mention all those aunts and grandmothers, he should have known what would come next—and as soon as her hands began to move he did know. They darted first to her hair, then scrambled down the front of her, touching spots and smudges, some of them real. "Mike! I can't! Look at me!"

"I *am* looking at you!" He gave the backpack another shrug and picked up her bundle too. Suddenly he felt terrific. He could have carried a hundred bundles. He was ten feet tall and two yards wide, and he had the world in his left hip pocket.

"You look great!" he said. "You look like the prettiest gargoyle anywhere! Come on—let's go."

For an instant she hesitated, then she put her hand in the one he held out to her, and they started down the long stairway just as the bells in the tower high above them pealed out to tell the ancient island that another day was drawing to a close.

About the Author

William Corbin needs little introduction. He is the author of many fine books for young people. Among them are *Smoke, Golden Mare*, both winners of the Pacific Northwest Library Association Young Readers Choice Award, and *High Road Home*, awarded the Child Study Association honor award in 1955. With his most recent works, *The Everywhere Cat* and *The Day Willie Wasn't*, Mr. Corbin has created two delightful picture books for the very young.

Born in Des Moines, Iowa, Mr. Corbin was educated at Principia College, the University of Missouri, Drake University, and Harvard. For many years he worked as a newspaperman in Ohio, Oklahoma, and California.

Mr. Corbin and his wife, Eloise Jarvis McGraw, live in a house atop Indian Mountain in Lake Oswego, Oregon, from which they have a spectacular view of Mount Hood.